# Sticks and Strings
## A Boy and His Bow

### Jimmy Tidmore

Fourth Installment in The Hunt Club Kids Series

Join the club at HuntClubKids.com

*Sticks and Strings: A Boy and His Bow*

Copyright © 2023 Jimmy Tidmore

Book Cover Design by ebooklaunch.com

Hardcover ISBN: 979-8-9895357-1-2
Paperback ISBN: 979-8-9895357-0-5
eBook ISBN: 979-8-9867159-9-5

Jimmy Tidmore Books LLC
6585 Hwy 431 S Suite E #183
Hampton Cove, AL 35763

In memory of and with much appreciation to G. Fred Asbell. He didn't know me, but I felt I knew him—thanks to his books.

# Chapter 1

I could tell by the whispering coming from the kitchen that something was wrong. I wasn't sure how long they had been in there, but it seemed like forever—an hour, at least. And I knew that the longer it went on, the worse it had to be.

I was trying to listen to them over the TV, but I knew if I turned the volume down any lower, it would be obvious. Eventually, my mom hurried past me through the living room. When she did, I knew my suspicions were correct. While she didn't say a word, the look on her face told me more than I wanted to know—something was definitely wrong, and it was a pretty big deal.

My dad followed her from the kitchen but couldn't keep up. She was moving back toward their bedroom, and she was moving fast. It was obvious that she wanted to be alone, so he let her go. His breath was coming out as one long sigh after another. And his hands were behind his head, which was looking down toward the floor.

I didn't want to stare at him, but it was hard not to. I could tell he was upset, but I wasn't sure if I was supposed to say anything. So, I just sat there with my head turned toward the TV while my eyes remained turned toward him.

Right when the silence was becoming awkward, he made his way over to the sofa and sat down beside me. I quickly glanced back over to the TV and acted like I hadn't been watching him. Dad didn't say anything at first. He just kept staring down at the floor, probably thinking about what he was going to say and how he was going to say it. And then, when I wasn't sure I could take it anymore, he broke the silence, saying, "Son, we need to talk."

He didn't raise his head at first, and I could tell by his voice that while we needed to talk, he didn't really want to. While I wasn't certain about what he had to say, I was certain that I didn't want to hear it. But all sorts of bad things were running through my head—and I had to know. So, I looked over at him and said, "Okay, about what?"

"Well, something not too good happened today, Parker. I got some news that's going to affect us all—you, me, your mom, and your sister, too. It's going to mean a lot of changes for us."

Changes? I didn't want any changes. I liked things the way they were. And based on the way my mom just ran past me, I was pretty sure that whatever these changes were, they weren't good. And no matter how hard my dad tried for the next twenty minutes or so to make them sound good, I eventually got up and ran to my room just like my mom had done.

# Chapter 2

"I still can't believe he had a mohawk!" Jet shouted when Mason finished telling us the story about killing his first turkey.

"I wouldn't have believed it either, Jet. I ain't ever seen anything like it," Mason replied with his thick southern drawl.

"We told you turkey hunting was awesome," Wyatt added. "You didn't even believe us at first. You said they were just stupid ol' birds that weren't worth chasing!"

"Yeah, well, I was the stupid one," Mason admitted. "Turkey hunting is every bit as fun as deer hunting. It really gets your heart pumping! I almost passed out a couple of times," he added with a laugh.

Turkey season had just ended the week-end before, which meant it was time for the next Hunt Club Kids meeting in Wyatt's treehouse. The other boys were having a good time talking about Mason's turkey. But I wasn't even sure why I was here. With the news my dad had dropped on us this week, what was the point? In a few months, they'd be having these meetings without me. And who knows what I'd be doing?

I still couldn't believe it. I couldn't imagine my dad doing this to us. But he was. And while I knew he was sad about it, too, I'm not sure anyone else in the family was as up-set as me. These guys were the best friends a boy could have, and no matter what my parents said, I'd never have others like them. NEVER! And so, I wasn't just sad. I was also mad—mad at my dad and even mad at my mom because she was letting it happen.

As I was thinking about all this again, Wyatt interrupted my thoughts when he tossed a Moon Pie to each of us and said, "Hey guys, my dad wanted me to talk to y'all about something."

"Was it that we better have a good dentist to go to tomorrow morning after eating all this sugar?" Mason asked with a snarky smile.

"No! But you ain't got to eat it!" Wyatt fired back.

"Yeah," Jet added. "Toss it to me! I'd hate for you to get a cavity."

"No, seriously, guys!" Wyatt started again. "My dad wanted me to ask you about doing a group hunt out here this fall—you and all your dads."

"I'm in," Jet said without any hesitation.

"Yeah, buddy. Me too!" Mason agreed. "That monster buck's brother is probably walking around out here, and I'd be more than happy to take him home."

11

Mason was talking about the giant buck that Wyatt's dad had killed on their property this past December. Wyatt and his dog, Willie, had actually found one of the monster buck's sheds around this time last year. And getting that buck in their freezer (and on their wall) was all Wyatt and his dad had focused on leading up to last season. It really was a giant. It even made it into the record books, I think. So, an invite to hunt on the property where a buck like that had been killed was an opportunity that no one could pass by. Unless, of course, you wouldn't be around for it—like me!

"Well, talk to your dads and let us know. I guess they can get together and work out a date. But you're all in, right?" Wyatt asked, looking for a nod from each of us.

"Yep!" Jet said with a nod.

"You know it," Mason agreed.

But when Wyatt looked toward me, I didn't know what to say.

# Chapter 3

"Ummm... I'll ask my dad," I responded while doing my best not to look any of them in the eye. With all their eyes on me, that was the best I could come up with in the moment. When I did look up, I noticed they were all pretty confused by my response. I'm sure they were all wondering why I wasn't excited like them.

"Well, okay. Yeah, ask him," Wyatt replied with as much confusion in his voice as he was wearing on his face. "Yeah, ask him, Parker. I hope y'all can come," he continued, glancing at Mason and Jet to see if they were confused too. It was clear they were.

Feeling the awkwardness, Mason jumped in and changed the subject—thankfully, taking the attention off me. "Wyatt, tell us about your shed hunting. Have you found any big ones this year?" he asked.

"I've found some good ones," Wyatt answered. "Nothing like the big one I found last year, but I'm still looking. Who knows, maybe that monster buck does have a brother. What about you and your dad?" he continued, "Have y'all had any luck?"

"Well, you know," Mason began, "my dad sent Bella away to get her trained for duck hunting. So, I haven't been able to do anything with her. But we've found a few. Nothing to write home about, though."

Bella was the yellow Labrador Retriever Mason's dad bought last year after seeing how good Wyatt's Lab, Willie, was at shed hunting. But he had bought her for duck hunting too—which Mason had told us again and again he cared nothing about. "I'd just rather focus her on shed hunting. But my dad has gotten himself all interested in duck hunting. Which has to be the most boring kind of hunting there is," he complained.

"Kind of like turkey hunting?" Jet asked with a smirk on his face that was meant to remind Mason that before he tried it, he had once thought the same thing about turkey hunting.

"Yeah, yeah, yeah," Mason answered, knowing Jet was poking fun at him and that maybe he had a point. "But either way, I'd rather have Bella in the woods with me right now, searching for sheds instead of off at the trainer. I sure could use her help."

"Speaking of turkey hunting," Wyatt jumped in, "how'd your season end up, Jet?"

Jet went on to explain that both he and his dad had gotten gobblers on opening weekend, and then after striking out the rest of the season, his dad had gotten one more on the last day.

"My dad was going to let me shoot it, but we couldn't get it to come in close enough for my .410. And so, before it slipped away, he looked over at me, and I nodded, telling him it was okay for him to take it. About three seconds later, the big gobbler was flipping and flopping on the ground, and we were running toward it."

———

Those sorts of conversations continued for the rest of the night until we eventually all fell asleep—which couldn't come soon enough for me. Truth be told, I wasn't really interested in any of their hunting talk. My mind was on other things, and I really didn't feel like being there—nor pretending like I wanted to be. And so, I was ready for bed long before anyone else and thankful when everyone finally stopped talking.

I was ready for morning to come so I could get back home and do everything I could to maybe change my parents' minds.

# Chapter 4

"Why are you doing this to us, Dad? No one wants to do it but you! It isn't fair! I don't want to leave!" I shouted as soon as the truck door shut the next morning.

"Parker, I don't want to leave either," he answered in a much calmer tone than I had used. "I don't know where you got the idea that this is something I want to do. It's not. But I don't have a choice. I can't help that the company is moving our headquarters to Texas. It wasn't my decision. In fact, I'm fortunate that they even offered me the option to go with them. There are plenty of pilots in Texas."

My dad is a pilot for a large construction company in town that builds apartment buildings all over the country. This means he's gone a lot, constantly flying the people he works with to all the different cities where they have jobs going on.

"But Dad, I don't want to leave my friends! I don't want to leave our house, either. And what about baseball?" I continued.

"Parker," he said while turning out of Wyatt's driveway and onto the main road, "they have baseball in Texas. And you'll make new friends, son."

"I am so tired of everyone saying that!" I nearly shouted. "I don't want new friends. I'll never have other friends like the ones I have here."

"Listen, Parker, I really do understand," Dad answered. "My parents moved around a lot when I was a kid. So, believe it or not, I know how you're feeling. And I hate that it's happening. In fact, I moved around so much as a kid that I promised myself I would never do this to my own family. But I don't have any option, son. I don't know what else to do. I have to provide for our family. And flying is the only thing I can do at this point in life. I'm too far down the road to start a new career."

"But aren't there other flying jobs here? Aren't there other companies in town that need a pilot?" As those words were coming out of my mouth, I realized how brilliant they were! That was the solution! My dad just needed to find another company in town that needed a pilot. Surely, there had to be at least one! And then we could stay!

"Well, Parker, maybe—hopefully," he replied. "I haven't wanted to mention that possibility because I didn't want to get your hopes up. But when my boss told me last week, that was the first thing that came into my mind. And I've been asking around ever since. In fact, I don't have any trips scheduled for this coming week, and I plan to spend every minute of every day looking for any other company that might need a pilot. But I only have a week. I have to let my boss know my final decision next Monday."

"You'll find something, Dad! I know you will. And we won't have to move!" I shouted, feeling happy for the first time in almost a week.

"No, Parker. Don't get your hopes up. There aren't many jobs like mine out there. They are tough to come by, which is why I don't have an option about moving. If the company is moving, then we have to go with them."

"Unless you can find something else!" I butted in. "And you will, Dad! I know you will! You just have to!"

# Chapter 5

Before I knew it, we were pulling into our driveway, and the conversation continued as we walked into the house. My mom and my sister, Piper, were sitting at the kitchen table, looking at houses on my mom's tablet.

"Finding anything you like?" my dad asked.

"Yeah," Mom answered, "Piper and I have found one neighborhood that we really like."

"But we're not moving!" I interrupted with my good news. "All Dad has to do is find another flying job here in town!"

As I was saying it, my mom lifted her eyebrows and looked toward my dad as if to say, "I thought you weren't going to mention that to him?"

Dad apparently knew exactly what she was getting at because he answered, "He figured it out on his own. Didn't you, Parker?"

"Yes, I did. I just can't believe it took so long. It's such an easy solution to our problem," I replied.

"No, it's not, Parker. It's not easy at all," my sister answered me before going on to explain everything my dad had already said to me on the way home. "There just aren't going to be any companies in town looking for a pilot right now," she insisted.

"Yes, there are!" I insisted back. "There has to be! Because I'm not moving!"

Before Piper had a chance to answer, my mom gave her a look, telling her that was enough. "Piper, why don't we look some more later? I'll come up and get you in a little while, okay?" Which was Mom's way of saying it was time for my sister to go upstairs so that she and Dad could have another talk with me—another talk about the same old stuff I didn't want to hear anything else about.

Piper is fifteen years old—five years older than me. Like my dad, she is fascinated with airplanes and plans to be a pilot when she grows up. That's part of the reason why she is taking this easier than me. I've heard her and Dad talking about how good the flight school is in the town we are moving to in Texas. Apparently, the airport is nice, too, and Dad is talking about buying a plane for Piper to do her training in. I think he's just bribing her to go. But that's not going to work with me! Nothing is going to make me okay with this!

"Listen, honey," my mom began, motioning for me to sit down in the seat Piper had left, "I know this is a shock. And I know it isn't something you want to do. It's not really anything I want to do, either. But it's what we have to do. But I think if you'd let me show you the place we're going, you might get excited about it. They have a really good Little League. And you could get started with fall baseball in September. I'm sure you'd make a lot of friends really fast. And I truly believe that by this time next year, you'd love it just as much as you love it here."

"There's no way, Mom," I answered firmly. "There's just no way. I'm not moving."

She started to answer but looked up at my dad, asking for help.

"Listen, Parker," he said as he sat down across from me, "if there was anything I could do to change the situation, I would. I don't want to do this to any of us. But I really need you to get on board with this like your mom and sister have. You have to accept it and figure out a way to make the best of it. Being mad about it and sad about it isn't going to change anything, is it?"

"No, but you finding another job this week will!" I answered before he could continue. "Just promise me you're going to try, Dad. Just promise me you'll do whatever you can to find another job so that we can stay!"

"Okay, Parker, I promise," He answered. "But I need you to promise me something, too. Okay?"

After I nodded, he continued by saying, "If I keep my promise to you, and spend my every waking moment this next week looking for a flying job that will keep us here in town, I need you to promise that if that doesn't work out, that you'll try your hardest to accept what we are having to do, and try to have a better attitude about it. Can you do that?"

I sat and thought about what he said for several seconds. While I wasn't sure how I could ever feel any different about leaving, I knew only one answer would do. So, I said, "I'll do my best, Dad," before adding, "But I really, really, really want you to find a way that we can stay. Because I can't imagine leaving my friends—especially the Hunt Club Kids."

# Chapter 6

At church the next morning, when Sunday School was wrapping up, my teacher asked if there were any prayer requests like she does every week. I wasn't sure if I was supposed to share about my dad's job or not. But I was really upset about it and wanted to say something. So, I raised my hand and said, "I'm not sure if I am supposed to share this or not. But I'm so worried about it that I'm going to."

This brought a concerned look to Ms. Valerie's face. "Oh no, Parker. What is it?" she asked.

"Well," I began to explain, "my dad's company is moving to Texas. Which means that unless he can find another job this week, we're moving to Texas, too."

"Oh goodness, when?" she replied.

"Over the summer—so in just a few weeks, I guess," I answered her. "But I really, really don't want to go. I don't want to leave my friends, I don't want to leave my house, and now that I am here and thinking about it, I don't want to leave this church."

It was all I could do to keep myself from crying. And while I hadn't cried about it at all yet, I had felt like it many times.

When she saw I was upset, Ms. Valerie slid her seat over close to mine and put her arm around me. "I know that's hard, Parker. I'm so sorry. How can we pray for you?"

"Well, please pray that my dad will be able to find another job this week so that we can stay. But I guess also pray that if he doesn't, that it wouldn't be too bad—the move and all. Pray that I'd be able to find some new friends and go to a good school and all that."

"It's scary, isn't it?" Ms. Valerie asked.

And with that, my eyes filled with tears, and all I could do was lower my head and nod.

"Kids," Ms. Valerie said as she patted me on the back, "will you please pray for Parker this week?"

"Yes, ma'am," I heard again and again—which made me feel better. And Ms. Valerie's prayer at the end of class made me feel even better. Surely, I thought, God will listen and answer if this many people are praying about it. Surely, we won't have to move.

---

What I didn't think about when I shared that prayer request in Sunday School is that while none of my Hunt Club Kids friends go to church with me, other kids from our school do. And so, when I arrived at school the next morning, I quickly found out the news about my dad's job had beaten me there. Wyatt, Jet, and Mason had beaten me there, too. And they were all waiting for me as soon as I walked in the door.

"Why didn't you tell us?" Wyatt demanded. "That's why you were so quiet the other night, isn't it?"

"You could have told us," Mason joined in.

"Yeah, you could have told us," Jet said. "We didn't know what was going on with you."

"I know, guys. I know," I began to explain myself. "I just really didn't want to talk about it the other night. I just didn't feel like it. It really stinks, and I really don't want to go."

"So, when are you moving?" Mason asked.

"Well," I continued, "if my dad can't find another job this week, we plan to move over the summer. My parents want us settled before my sister and I start school out there this fall."

"But summer is just a few weeks away!" Jet shouted.

"Yeah, I know," I answered. "I just can't believe it."

"But there's still a chance y'all might stay?" Wyatt asked. "There's still a chance that your dad will find a job, and you won't have to go?"

"Well, there's a chance," I answered. "But my dad says it's not very likely. There just aren't many companies in town who are going to be looking for pilots right now. And he says there's nothing else he can do. All he's done since college is fly airplanes, and it would be too tough for him to do something different now. So, it looks like we're going. It looks like we're going to Texas whether I want to or not."

It's sort of funny that in the same way my parents weren't wanting me to get my hopes up, I didn't want my friends to get theirs up, either. So, I played down the possibility that my dad might find another job. But truthfully, my hopes were sky-high that morning. Because after dropping me off at school, my dad was headed out to the airport to check with some of his pilot friends about jobs with their companies. And I knew that when I got home that day, he'd have some good news.

He just had to!

# Chapter 7

When I saw my mom's van coming through the carpool line, I couldn't wait to get in and ask her about it. All I wanted was for things to go back to normal. And they couldn't get back to normal until I knew for certain we weren't going to Texas.

But, when the side door on the van slid open, and I jumped into one of the backseats, my mom beat me to it. "I know you're going to ask," she said, "but I haven't heard anything from your dad. He's been gone all day, and I know he's doing everything he can to keep his promise to you—

about trying to find a job that would keep us here."

"But," she continued after a short pause, "I also want to remind you that you made a promise to him. And so, I want you to be working toward that in your mind. Because, as much as we all hope that your dad can find something that will keep us from having to move, that is probably just not going to happen, Parker. And he feels bad enough about that already. When things don't work out—after all the effort he's put in to keep his promise to you—he certainly doesn't need you making him feel worse. Okay? Do you understand what I'm trying to say?"

I understood. So, I said, "Yes, ma'am. I understand. But I really think he's going to find something. I really do. He's got all week. Surely, he can find something."

"Well, I know he is going to try," she answered. "But I want you to promise me that you are going to try to accept the fact that it's probably not going to happen, and we'll probably have to move. And I want you to try to accept that it's not going to be the end of the world. I know it's hard to leave your friends, your school, your house, and your church—everything you have ever known. But you'll still be with your family, Parker. And we'll be back for holidays to visit your grandparents. And I promise that whenever we come, we'll work it out so that you can spend time with your friends. They'll always be your friends, Parker. And you can stay in touch with them on the phone."

Yeah, but it would never be the same. I didn't say it out loud because I had said it a hundred times already. Instead, I said, "Okay. If things don't work out, I'll do my best to have a better attitude about it."

Even though I said it, I didn't really know how it would be possible. I still couldn't imagine it. And there was no way I was ready to accept it. Dad just had to come through. He had to find something that would let us stay.

――――――――

When mom turned into the driveway, I was stretching to get a look over the front seats, hoping to see my dad's truck parked in front of the garage. But his spot was empty. Which meant he hadn't found anything yet. But it also meant he hadn't given up and that there was still hope.

Apparently, I was the only one in the family who still had any hope, though. Because when I made it inside, there were boxes everywhere. Mom had spent her day packing! She had given up! And it made me furious.

"Mom! Why are you packing? It's not a done deal yet!" I said angrily.

"Honey," she replied, "it pretty much is. That's what we've been trying to tell you."

I knew that I was going to get in trouble if I said anything else—because I knew it wouldn't be nice. So, I picked up my back-pack, grabbed a snack, and ran up the stairs to my room.

But when I turned the corner and walked through the doorway, I couldn't believe she had been in there packing some of my stuff, too!

"No!" I shouted where she could hear it. "No, no, no!" I screamed as I looked at the boxes. I was so angry I could hardly control myself. But I made my way over to the boxes and began unpacking everything—putting it back where it belonged! It took me ten or fifteen minutes, I guess, and I was so into what I was doing that I didn't notice my dad standing in the doorway, watching me have my little fit.

"Hey buddy," he said with a sad smile on his face when I eventually looked over and noticed him.

"Hey, Dad," I replied, embarrassed that he had been watching.

He walked in and sat down on my bed, patting it as a sign for me to sit down, too.

"How'd it go today?" I asked as I sat down next to him.

"Uhhh…. about like I expected, I guess. Not much luck."

"But you have the rest of the week," I reminded him.

"Yeah, I do. But it's going to be hard," he said as a reminder to me.

"But you're going to keep trying, right?" I hoped out loud.

"Of course I am. I promised you I would. And I will not give up until I have done everything I can do to find something that will keep us from having to move. But," he continued after a short pause, "at some point, I will have done everything I can do. And then, it'll be time for you to keep the promise you made to me. Right?"

# Chapter 8

He was right. So, I agreed. But I still didn't know how I'd be able to do it. And I still wasn't giving up on him finding a new job here—one that would let us stay put.

As day after day passed, though, with my dad continuing to come home each night with no good news, reality was starting to set in. And I was slowly starting to accept the fact that we would be moving to Texas.

When I woke up Saturday morning, Dad was already gone—and I was up pretty early. "He has this one last day to find a job," my mom explained. "So, he's back out at the airport asking around and trying to have some meetings. He has to give his boss a firm answer on Monday, and tomorrow, we'll be at church. So, this is it," she explained.

I tried to enjoy the day but couldn't. All I could think about was where my dad was and what he was doing. And truthfully, I was starting to feel bad that he was doing it all for me. I knew he was at this point. Even though they were trying to hide it, I could tell that Mom and Piper were sort of excited about the move. While Piper would be leaving her friends, too—just like I was—it didn't seem to bother her as much as it bothered me. She said she'd be leaving them in a couple of years anyway when she headed to college. And I had heard Mom say that she knew she and my dad would end up back here someday—certainly when he retired—so she wouldn't really be losing any of her friends, "just taking a little vacation from them—that's all."

Of course, that's not how I felt. I was miserable over leaving my friends. And I knew things would never be the same for me. And yet, by the time the sun started down that Saturday evening, I had accepted in my heart and mind that the move to Texas was going to happen and that it would be okay.

When my dad got home that night with no good news for us, he looked as defeated as I had ever seen him. It made me feel bad that I had been so selfish and that I had made him go through all that he did this past week—even when he knew how it was going to turn out.

And so, when Mom and Piper headed upstairs to put some more of their things in boxes, I was happy to have a moment alone with my dad—to tell him about my change of heart. Of course, I told him that I was still sad about the move but that I was ready to keep my promise to him, just as he had kept his promise to me. "As long as you can help me find a good baseball team, I'll be good, Dad. And as long as you promise that whenever we come back, I can see my friends, it'll all be okay."

That brought a big smile to his face—a smile I hadn't seen from him all week. "That's a deal, Parker. We'll get you on the best baseball team in town, and we'll make sure to get you back here as much as we can, maybe even for a couple of weeks each summer."

That made me smile, too. And after watching a funny show together as a family, we all went to bed that night, content with the situation and ready for whatever was ahead of us in the days and weeks to come.

# Chapter 9

In Sunday School the next day, I gave everyone an update and told them that we would be moving after all—that my dad had tried as hard as he could to find a way for us to stay, but that it just didn't work out. At the end of class, Ms. Valerie prayed for me and said we would have a class party before I went away.

On the way home from church, Wyatt's mom called my mom and invited me to come over. She said the other Hunt Club Kids were coming over, too, and that they were all worried this might be the last time for the four of us to get together. They talked for a little bit longer, and while I couldn't hear the whole conversation, I did hear my mom say, "Yes, it's a done deal at this point. We've decided to go, and he'll be telling his boss tomorrow."

My dad was driving, and even though I was sitting behind him, I noticed the expression on his face change as my mom said it. I could tell it was still bothering him. But we all knew there was nothing else to do. He had tried everything he could do to find a way for us to stay, but it just wasn't meant to be.

———————

After a quick stop at home for me to change into some play clothes, Mom and I were back outside and climbing into the van for the trip over to Wyatt's house. Piper had some homework to do, and Dad said he was heading out to the airport to get some things in the hangar packed away for the move to

Texas. He waved as we backed out, and I heard him holler for me to have a good time.

The other Hunt Club Kids were right. This probably would be the last time we'd be together before I left Alabama for Texas. Things were starting to move fast now, and our house was already halfway packed up in boxes. School was about to be done, and Mom and Dad had pretty well zeroed in on a new house in the town we'd be moving to.

Me and the rest of the guys all agreed that while I would be away, I would still be an official member of the Hunt Club Kids. We did decide and vote for Mason to replace me as president. We also discussed ways for me to continue meeting with them virtually from time to time so that I could keep up with what was going on with them, and they could keep up with what was going on with me. We even talked about expanding the club as I met some new friends who hunted out in Texas.

"Dad says there's good huntin' out there, Parker," Mason happily explained. "You ain't going to be missing out on nothin' there."

"Yeah, but I'll definitely miss all of you," I said back, giving them all a brief look.

Everyone was quiet for several seconds before Jet said, "We'll miss you too, Parker. But you ain't gone forever. And we'll all still be able to talk to each other from time to time. Plus, didn't your mom say you could come visit us for a few weeks each summer?"

---

The conversations in Wyatt's treehouse that afternoon bounced back and forth between hunting and me moving. And while I still had several more days with them at school, we all knew that there was something very final about this day. It would be the last time The Hunt Club Kids—the original four at least—gathered together like this for one of our regular meetings. It was hard to believe that it was coming to an end. But it was, and we all knew it. No matter what our plans were about getting together in the future, things would be different from this point forward.

Then, before we knew it, our parents started arriving to pick us up. One by one, each of the other boys shook my hand and patted me on the shoulder. None of us really knew what to say, but we all knew what the other was thinking. I loved these guys and was going to miss them. I was going to miss them a lot.

# Chapter 10

"Unpack the boxes! We're not moving!"

I had been home from Wyatt's for about an hour when the door burst open, and my dad came barreling through it, screaming those words over and over again as he ran from one room to another.

"Unpack the boxes! We're not moving!"

Piper and I ran downstairs and saw Mom running out of the kitchen. She had a roll of packing tape in one hand, and the other hand was covering her mouth, which was wide open in shock.

"What do you mean we're not moving?!?!" she asked in excitement. "What do you mean?" she asked again.

"You're just not going to believe it!" my dad answered. "I can hardly believe it myself," he said while collapsing onto the sofa and burying his face into his hands.

By this point, Piper and I were curious and excited, too.

"Come on, Dad, tell us!" Piper insisted.

"Yeah, I can't stand it anymore!" I pleaded in agreement.

"For real! Stop messing around and tell us," Mom said as she plopped down beside him and started shaking his shoulder.

"Well," he answered, lifting his head from his hands, "something crazy happened this afternoon while I was out at the airport. It happened so fast that I am still trying to process it. But the good news is that we're not going to be moving. We're staying right here."

"But how?" my mom asked, desperately wanting more details. "Did you finally find a company looking for a pilot?"

"No," he answered proudly. "I found something better."

"You're killing us, Dad," Piper shouted. "Just tell us!"

"Okay, okay," he gave in. "I'm getting to it," he said with a smile.

"So, while I was out at the airport today," Dad continued as we all leaned in closer, "I walked by one of the hangars down toward the end of the runway—the ones that have been there for a while and look like it. I hadn't checked them out before because I didn't really think I'd find a company with a plane based out of one of those hangars. They were just too small and too old for that. But, seeing that I had tried everything else and that this was my last day to search and all, I knew I had nothing to lose by checking to make sure. So, I walked down that way, and I found one hangar with the big door open. There was an old man inside picking through some stuff. It caught my attention because none of it was airplane stuff. In fact, there wasn't an airplane in the hangar at all. It was a bunch of wood and just some old equipment of some sort. That seemed kind of weird to me, and, I guess, without even knowing it, I stopped and watched him for a bit—curious about what he was doing."

He had all our attention now, and I was dying to know what this had to do with us not having to move.

"Well," Dad continued, "I'm not sure how long I stood there, but eventually, the old man noticed me. And said, 'Hey there! How are you doing?' It honestly caught me off guard, and I didn't know what to say. So, I just told the truth and answered him, saying, 'Well, I was just walking by and got curious as to what you were doing. I could tell none of this was airplane stuff, and that got my attention, I guess.'"

"Naw, it certainly ain't airplane stuff," the man told my dad. "I know the guy who runs the airport, and he's let me rent one of these old hangars for several years—sort of under the radar. It was a lot cheaper for me than renting a real storage building, so I really appreciated it. But he called me last week and said that they were going to be tearing these old hangars down in a few months to build new ones and that I'd have to get my stuff out in the next month or two. And so, I came down here today to make a plan, I guess. I'm just not sure what I ought to do with all of it. It kind of means a lot to me—which is why I have held onto it for all these years."

"Well, come to find out," my dad continued his story, "the stuff in the hangar was the remains of his old archery business. He used to build custom bows for people—really nice stuff, not the kind of bows you'd buy in a store. But true works of art—traditional longbows and recurves that he handmade out of all different kinds of wood. He showed me some pictures he had kept in an old binder. It's crazy that someone could build bows that looked so nice and still shot so well, according to him."

"So, what's this got to do with us and with your job situation?" my mom asked, with a concerned tone in her voice. "What does any of this have to do with us not having to move?" she continued, almost demanding an answer.

"Well, that's just it," my dad began to explain, "we're now in the archery business!"

# Chapter 11

"Oh my, oh my, oh my," my mom said while jumping up from the sofa to pace around the room while nervously running her hands through her already messed-up hair. "We don't know the first thing about running an archery business," she worried out loud as she continued to pace. "We don't know a thing about making or selling bows! We'll go broke!" she insisted while staring at the floor as she paced around the room that was full of the boxes we had been busy packing all day.

"But that's just it," my dad answered, standing up and walking over to her, "Forrest is going to help us. After I talked to him for a while and explained what was going on with us—including why I was out at the airport looking into other people's hangars—he said, 'Well, that's a shame you've gotta move your family like that. Just as much of a shame as me having to get rid of all this equipment that means so much to me."

Dad went on to explain that Forrest was the old man's name—Forrest Gentry—and that after talking about both their situations for a while, Mr. Forrest offered to sell my dad all the equipment. "And not only that," Dad said, trying to convince my mom about his crazy plan, "he even offered to work alongside me for a while to help me get the business back up and going. He said he'd stay on as long as I needed and would step away when the time was right. He's going to show me everything I need to know to get the business up and going again."

"Surely, to heavens, you said 'No!'" my mom begged. "Please tell me that's not why we're staying! We don't know anything about running an archery business! There has to be another reason!" she said desperately.

After a brief pause, where it was obvious he was thinking about how to answer, Dad said, "No. That's it. That was my plan. I sort of felt like it just fell into my lap and that it was the only option I had to keep us from having to move. But, if you don't think it's a good idea, I'll call him and back out."

Well, I still really didn't want to move, and the idea of my dad owning an archery business was cooler than I could handle, so without even thinking about it, I shouted, "This is so awesome! I can't believe we're not moving! And I can't believe you're buying a bow-making business!"

After looking over toward me and smiling, I saw my dad glance at my mom, who had also turned her head to look at me. That's when Piper jumped in and said, "I think it's cool too, Dad. And you can figure it out. You might not know what you're doing right now, but if you can land an airplane, you can build a bow. I say go for it!"

With that, the mood in the room began to change. And we all looked at my mom, who was staring back down at the floor again—clearly thinking. She slowly walked back over to the sofa and sat down next to my dad again. The suspense was killing us like it had been before. I felt like my whole future was dangling from a string.

"Okay, then," she looked up and said, moving her eyes from my dad's, then to Piper's, and finally to mine, "if y'all are all onboard, I am too. I surely don't want to move, and if this is God's answer, then it's his answer. And, of course, if it is his answer, then I know it'll work out."

After slapping his hands together with excitement, Dad went on to explain how that he really did think it was God's answer. He talked about how he had prayed on the way out to the airport for God to give him any sort of opportunity to keep us from having to move. He said, "I told him I was willing to do whatever—even something crazy if that's what it took. In fact, I was praying that very thing as I walked around the corner of Mr. Forrest's hangar. So yes, there's no doubt that this is a pretty crazy idea. But I really do feel like God has given this to us. And I really do believe that if we all work together as a family, we can make it go."

# Chapter 12

Before leaving the next morning, we had a pretty serious meeting at the breakfast table. We had been thinking about this day for two weeks now. It was the Monday my dad had to tell his boss his final decision. And before he left for that meeting, and before Piper and I left for school, he wanted to give us all—Mom included—one final chance to back out.

"Listen," he said, "we're either all in this together, or we are not in it at all. This is a big decision—one that is going to affect the whole family. What we are about to do will require every one of us to be on board and ready to work hard to make it successful. And so, before I let my boss know that we won't be coming with them to Texas, I want to hear from you all one last time. You've had the night to sleep on it. So, are you still on board?"

First, he turned toward me, looking for an answer. "No doubt," I answered with a nod or two. "Let's do it, Dad."

"Same for me," Piper answered as he turned toward her. "Is it kind of crazy? Yeah, but so is moving to Texas, right in the middle of high school. So, let's build some bows!"

Then, it was my mom's turn. I was honestly a little worried that she might have changed her mind. It was kind of a crazy idea. I was only ten, but I knew enough to know that. But, with every eye on her, Mom looked to my dad and said, "I'm in. There's no doubt it's crazy, but we're kind of crazy too. So, it might be a perfect fit!" she said with a laugh and a smile.

And with that, my dad was out the door, and we were off to school.

---

The Hunt Club Kids couldn't believe it.

"Wait, you're not moving?!?!" Wyatt asked excitedly after I explained to them what had happened yesterday.

"And your dad is opening an archery business?" Jet asked, joining in on the excitement.

"Yep!" I happily answered them both. "We're staying put, and we're opening a custom bow-making business."

"But how?" Mason asked. "I don't mean to be mean, but does your dad know how to build a bow?"

Mason had never been mean a minute in his life, so it was funny to hear him worry that I'd take it that way.

"I know you're not being mean, Mason. You've never been mean to anyone. Honestly, it's a good question. My mom asked it a hundred times last night. But no, my dad hasn't ever built a bow—he doesn't have a clue how to do it. None of us do. Which is why the guy he's buying all the equipment from is going to help us get started. He's going to show us everything we need to know, and once we have it up and going, he'll step away and leave it to us."

"That's just too cool," Jet jumped back in. "What are you going to call it? What's the name of the business going to be?"

That was a good question, too, because I don't think anyone in my family had even thought about that.

"You know… we haven't even thought about it," I answered. "I guess we might start talking about that tonight. My dad is going to see his old boss today to let him know that we won't be moving to Texas. But the plan for tonight is for us to run out to the airport so that we can all meet Mr. Forrest and begin making plans about getting everything moved out of the hangar to wherever we are going to put it."

"Where are you going to put it?" Mason asked.

"That I don't know, either," I admitted. "After meeting with his boss today, Dad is going to start looking for a building we can rent—one that is big enough for all the equipment and for everything else we need to run the business. And once he has that, we'll rent a big truck and start moving everything."

"Jet's right, Parker. This is super cool," Wyatt jumped back in. "And I'm super happy you're not moving. Things just wouldn't have been the same here without you."

"I'm happy too," I agreed. "And getting to help my dad with the bow business is going to be great."

But now that Jet had asked, I couldn't stop thinking about what the name of the new business would be.

# Chapter 13

When I got home from school that afternoon and asked my parents about what we would name the business, they looked at me as cluelessly as I had looked at Jet when he had asked me the same question earlier that day.

"That's a good question, buddy," my dad admitted.

"And a pretty important one," Mom agreed.

"I guess I've been so caught up with the excitement of it all that I haven't even thought about needing a name," Dad explained. "Kind of embarrassing to admit, but it's true. It hasn't even crossed my mind."

"What did Mr. Forrest call his business?" I asked.

"Nothing special," Dad explained. "It was just Gentry Custom Bows. Gentry is his last name," Dad reminded me.

"Yeah… that's boring," Piper chimed in as she walked into the kitchen.

"I agree," Mom answered. "We have to come up with something better than that. I'm not banking our future on a business with a boring name."

———————

As we drove to the airport to meet Mr. Forrest, the conversation about the business name continued. Everyone was throwing out this suggestion and that, but no one came up with anything we liked. Most were boring: "Backwoods Bows," "Build-A-Bow," "The Better Bow Company," and so forth.

Some were silly: "Parker's Projectile Pushers," "Piper's Pigeon Poppers," and "Dad's Deer Destroyers." And those were the good ones.

It was fun to kid and laugh again after the past two weeks. With today's deadline looming over our heads, none of us had thought about anything else—certainly not anything fun or funny. But that was all behind us now. Dad had said that his boss was very nice about it all, even saying, "I envy what you're doing. And I hope it goes well for you. If not, we'll make a position for you in Texas. Everyone here loves you, and we'll be rooting for you. In fact, I want to be your first customer. When you have things up and going, give me a call, and I'll place an order. I need a new bow anyway."

"That sure was nice," my mom said after Dad told us about the conversation. "And at least we have a safety net should things not turn out the way we hope."

"Don't say that, Mom!" Piper protested. "It's going to go great!"

"Yeah, I know, honey, but it still makes me a little nervous," Mom admitted.

--------

After twenty minutes of driving, we made it to the airport. Dad stretched the security card on his neck out the car window and waved it at the box in front of the gate that led to the hangars. The box beeped, and the gate began to slide open.

After passing through the gate and following a narrow road to the end of the runway, where the old hangars were, we made a couple of more turns before coming to a hangar with an opened door.

"Here we are," Dad said as he put the car in park. "I know you know, Parker. But 'yes sir' and 'no sir' when Mr. Forrest speaks to you. Understand?"

"Yes, sir," I replied as we all stepped out and headed toward the hangar.

Before we could even get halfway from my mom's car to the hangar, a tall, skinny man made his way out. He was wearing dark gray pants and an old plaid shirt. He also had an odd-looking hat on his head with a feather in it.

"Well, hello there," he said as we were walking toward him. "Who are all these folks with you?" he asked, looking at my dad.

"Well, these are my business partners," Dad said with a smile. "Without them, none of this is going to work."

"You're right about that," Mr. Forrest replied. "It's going to take all of you. But, if you are all serious about it, I truly believe this will work out. I really do. I wouldn't have convinced you to do this if I didn't believe it. If I wasn't so old, I'd do it myself. Because there's a group of people out there today who are tired of all the gizmos and gadgets—the stuff all the big hunting companies want you to think you have to have. There are plenty of hunters ready to get back to our hunting roots. And there is no better way to do that than with traditional archery and traditional bowhunting," Mr. Forrest said, looking at me with a knowing smile.

"And who is this little guy right here?" he asked, walking over my way with his hand stuck out for a shake.

"I'm Parker," I answered as he grabbed my hand.

"We'll, Parker, it's nice to meet you. I think your dad says you and I are going to be working together. Is that right?" Mr. Forrest asked, looking back over at my dad.

"Yes, sir. Parker is going to be your right-hand man, Mr. Forrest. I want him to know everything about this business, from inside and out."

"And what about these two lovely ladies you got with you?" Mr. Forrest asked as he tipped his head toward my mom and sister. "I'm guessing these two are going to be the real brains behind the operation."

"Well, you've got that right, too," my dad answered with a laugh. "My wife is going to be in charge of anything and everything related to money. And my daughter, Piper," he continued with a nod toward my sister, "she's going to be in charge of everything related to social media and the Internet."

"Well, I don't know anything about that Internet, but it seems like all the young folks do," Mr. Forrest answered. "And if you're really after what I'm after with this little venture—exposing young folks to the old ways—you're going to need someone like your daughter who knows how to get the word out to them."

"I couldn't agree more," my dad answered. "You're right. A lot of folks are tired of all the gizmos and gadgets. They're longing for something simple and effective. And that's what this whole business is going to be about. But we're going to need your help, Forrest. We're really going to need your help."

"Well, sir, you have it. As long as you need it, you'll have it. But I suspect you'll be running things much better than I did in just a short while. All I knew was how to build bows. I wasn't so great at running a business. I can teach you how to build bows— I'm not worried about that at all. And between the four of you, I have no doubt that the business side of things will be running like a well-oiled machine in no time."

"I hope you're right, Mr. Forrest," my mom answered. "Because we're really taking a leap of faith here—really stepping out there and taking a big risk."

"Yes, ma'am, you are," Mr. Forrest answered her. "Yes, ma'am, you are."

# Chapter 14

"But first things first," Mr. Forrest said as he looked away from my mom, back toward me and my sister. "Have either of you ever shot a real bow before? Not one of those things with the training wheels, but an old-fashioned wooden bow without all those moving parts that squeak and break."

"Not me," Piper answered.

"Well, we're about to fix that," Mr. Forrest replied. "We're about to fix that right now," he continued as he walked over to a workbench and took out a beautiful long-bow from a long fleece sock. "This ought to work out for you just fine," he explained as he strung it up and handed it to her.

The stringing process involved resting the lower tip of the bow against his foot and bending the whole bow back across his leg until the upper loop of the bowstring settled into place on the bow's upper limb tip. I'd later find out this was pretty hard to do, but Mr. Forrest made it look easy.

"See if you can pull that back easy enough," he said to Piper as he handed her the bow. "But don't draw it back and just let it go," he warned as he helped her get her hands in place. "Doing that without an arrow is called dry firing," he explained. "And it can ruin a bow."

Piper was able to pull the bow back easily and even hold it for a while, with Mr. Forrest watching and saying, "Hold it... hold it... hold it. Good. Now let it down slowly."

Mr. Forrest took a step back from her and said, "Yes, ma'am. I think that'll work just fine. How 'bout you?"

"Yes, sir. That wasn't hard at all," she answered.

"Nor is it supposed to be," he insisted. "It don't take that much to kill a deer with a bow if you've got sharp broadheads and good flying arrows. Of course, we men have ego problems, which means we like to show everyone how strong we are. And so, we tend to use bows that are really hard to pull back. You women folk are much smarter than that, though, and don't care anything about our silly competitions. And guess what? The deer don't care either," he laughed.

Piper's bow was awesome. So, I was excited when he left her with it, walked back over to the bench, and began to pull out another bow from a different fleece sleeve. I was excited because I was pretty sure this one was for me.

"So, what about you, Parker? Have you ever shot a bow?" he asked as he removed the bow from the sleeve and began to string it up, like he had done with Piper's.

Unlike Piper, I had shot a bow a few times—at Mason's house. So, I proudly answered, "Yes, sir. I've shot my friend's compound bow a few times," thinking that would impress him. But I didn't know that when he talked about bows with "training wheels" earlier, that's what he meant—compound bows. And, while I didn't know it yet, I soon would—Mr. Forrest didn't like compound bows.

"Well, I'm glad you survived it," he said. "You ever seen one of those things blow up? It's a scary sight," he continued.

I wasn't exactly sure what he was talking about and didn't really care. Because by the time he finished, the bow he had taken out for me was in my hand. It was the most beautiful thing I had ever seen. I was amazed that something you hunted with could be that pretty.

"Is it mine?" I asked without realizing it was coming out of my mouth.

"Parker!" my mom interrupted.

"Oh, ma'am, don't worry about it," Mr. Forrest jumped in and saved me. "He ain't the first boy under the age of a hundred to get infatuated with a bow."

"Well, asking like that was a little rude," she apologized.

"Ahhh, it's fine. I'd be excited about it too, if I were him," he answered my mom before turning back to me. "Yes, this one is all yours, Parker. What do you think about it?"

I didn't know what to say. I didn't even know Mr. Forrest. I had just met him five minutes ago, and he just gave me a bow!

"Thank you, Mr. Forrest! Thank you so very much!" were the words that eventually came out. "I just love it. I love it so much," I continued without ever taking my eyes off the bow.

"I thought you would," he replied. "And tomorrow after school, we'll start practicing. How does that sound?" he asked, looking at Piper and me. I think he was more excited than we were.

"That sounds great," she answered.

"Yes, sir. It does!" I agreed.

---

After giving us the bows, Mr. Forrest and my parents began to talk serious stuff about the business. They spent some time looking around at all the equipment and the different piles of wood that were in the hangar. And they talked about the different buildings my dad had looked at that day to become our new bow-building shop.

While my sister was excited about her bow, she wasn't nearly as excited as me. And so, she quickly laid hers back down on the workbench and began to look around the hangar with the grown-ups.

I was still fascinated with my new bow, though, and couldn't wait to shoot it. I also couldn't help but want to pull it back like Piper had done, to pretend like I was shooting. I had listened to what Mr. Forrest had said to Piper about not pulling the string back and just letting it go without an arrow. I also remembered Mason and his dad telling me the same thing when I shot Mason's bow at their house. So, I knew I had to be careful about that. And I was.

But, when I lifted the bow with my left hand and began to pull back on the string with my right hand, I quickly ran into a problem. I wasn't strong enough. I could only get it back maybe halfway. I tried again, and again, and again, but I just couldn't do it.

# Chapter 15

I didn't tell anyone about my problem because I was a little embarrassed. And I thought that maybe I was just a little tired or something. Surely, I'd be able to do it in the morning. And if not, maybe Mr. Forrest would tell me what I was doing wrong when we practiced tomorrow afternoon.

But the next morning was no different. I had taken my bow into my room with me the night before, and the first thing I did when I hopped out of bed that morning was grab it and try to pull it back. I must have tried five times and still couldn't get it back any further than halfway.

I worried about it all day at school. And I even made the mistake of telling the other Hunt Club Kids about my awesome new bow—leaving out the part about not being able to draw it back.

"Like an Indian bow?" Mason asked.

"I guess," I answered. "It's just a piece of wood with a leather grip. And it doesn't have those training wheels like your bow," I jabbed at him with a snarky smile.

"Huh?" he asked, not sure what I was talking about.

"That's what Mr. Forrest says about compound bows," I answered, still smiling so he'd know I was just playing. "He says they have training wheels to make it easy."

"Aw, hogwash!" Mason said, as he elbowed me on the shoulder. "Those ain't training wheels! They're called 'cams,'" he continued, elbowing me one more time.

"I know, I know," I answered. "I'm just messin' with you," I said, rubbing my arm.

Mason could shoot a bow better than most grown men. There was no denying that. He could probably be in the Olympics or something if it wouldn't interfere with his hunting.

"That sounds pretty cool, Parker," Wyatt joined in. "Can you bring it to the meeting next Friday? My dad has a target in the back-yard, and he could help us shoot it."

Of course, now I was in a pickle. School was letting out for the summer next week, and the Hunt Club Kids had decided to cel-ebrate finishing the fourth grade—and that I wouldn't be moving—with a sleepover in Wyatt's treehouse. And now they all wanted me to bring my bow—and not just that, they wanted me to shoot it! Which, of course, I couldn't do. I couldn't even pull it back!

"Uh, yeah. Sure, I can bring it," my mouth said before my brain could stop it. "It shoots really good. Y'all won't believe it," my stupid mouth continued while my brain was screaming at it to stop.

So now, I was really in trouble. And I knew I was going to need some help—and I'd need it fast. Thankfully, I was going to practice with Mr. Forrest that afternoon. Maybe he could show me what I was doing wrong.

———————

"Well, son, you ain't doin' nothing wrong," Mr. Forrest explained when I showed up at the new bow shop that afternoon.

After talking with Mr. Forrest last night, my mom and dad had decided to rent some space in an old, historical building in our town that used to be a cotton mill. There were fancy restaurants and all sorts of different shops and stores in this old mill—mostly the kind of girly stuff my mom and sister and all their friends liked. But, after meeting with the man who owned the building, my dad had signed the papers on a section of it that would be perfect for housing the equipment we were buying from Mr. Forrest. And so, my mom was excited to pick me and Piper up from school that afternoon to take us out there so we could see the progress they had made moving things in that day. Of course, I was excited because I really needed Mr. Forrest's help figuring out why I couldn't pull back the bow he had given me. And I knew he'd be there too.

"No, you ain't doing nothing wrong at all," he continued. "The draw weight on this bow is just a little too much for you right now. Honestly, I was a little worried about it when I gave it to you. I made this bow for my son back when he was a youngster. But when I got to thinking about it last night, he was a few years older than you are when I made it for him. So, I was a little worried about it being a bit too much for you to draw. But don't worry," he continued, "I came up with a plan in case this happened."

*Good*, I thought before asking, "So you can make it easier for me to pull back?"

"Well, I could. But that's not my plan," he began to explain. "My plan is to just make you a new one—from scratch. And I was thinking that while we're at it, we could make one that fits you a little better. Ain't no use in a kid your age having to shoot a bow that's sized for grown-ups. No, we'll make one just for you—probably with shorter limbs and a smaller grip so that it fits your hand better. How does that sound?"

"That sounds great, Mr. Forrest! But can we really do that?" I asked without really thinking about it.

"Well, I sure hope so!" he laughed, looking around at all the equipment that had been set up in our new shop that day. "If we can't build a bow, we ain't got no business being in the bow-making business, do we?"

When he said it that way, I knew he was right.

# Chapter 16

The new bow shop was really cool. It was still hard to believe this was happening. Just a few days ago, we were half-packed and ready to move to Texas. Now, we were not only staying put in Alabama but also opening up an archery business and setting up equipment to build bows. And the more we looked around at the new shop and talked about it, the more it made sense to us that we would put our bow shop in an old historical building like this because the bows we would be building would be old and historical as well.

Over the past few days, I had come to understand that the types of bows we'd make were called traditional bows, which is why we kept trying to come up with a name for the business that had the word "traditional" in it. But we still hadn't come up with one we all liked or anything that made sense. That was about to change, though.

As we were looking around that afternoon, we made our way over to the part of the building where all the pieces of wood we'd use for making bows had been stacked. Mr. Forrest said these pieces of wood were called "staves." Across from these stacked wooden staves were rolls and rolls of string that he said he would soon teach us how to weave together into bowstrings. "They're called Flemish Twist strings," he explained as he grabbed a finished one to show us.

And that's when mom came up with the name for the business—without even knowing it. After looking at the stacks of staves, neatly organized on shelves, and after glancing over to the rolls of string that we would eventually weave into finished bowstrings, she looked over at my dad with a smile and said, "When you stand here and look at it all, it's kind of crazy to think that we've spent our life savings and are banking our future on nothing more than a bunch of sticks and strings."

As soon as the words came out of her mouth, my dad's eyes got really big. My mom's did, too. "That's it," they said at the same time.

"Yeah, that's it," Mr. Forrest agreed. "That's what you need to call your business. You need to call it Sticks and Strings."

Piper and I loved it, too. And it really made sense. Because traditional bows really aren't anything more than a stick and a string. And so, Sticks and Strings it was. Which meant we had a building, we had a name, and now we had work to do—beginning with building a new bow for me.

Mr. Forrest and I explained our bow-building plans to my dad. Fortunately, there was still plenty of organizational work for my parents to do around the shop, and according to my dad, "lots of other stuff to get done before we officially get going. So y'all go ahead," Dad said. "Plus," he continued, "it'll be good for Parker to learn about the bow-building process from beginning to end. It'll also be good for his bow to be one that he helped build."

And so, after spending a little time setting up a twenty-yard range in the far corner of the new shop and then spending some more time helping Piper practice with the bow he had given her last night, it was time for Mr. Forrest and me to get started on my new bow.

"Alright, son," he explained as we stood there looking at the stack of wooden staves that were neatly laid out before us. There are lots of different kinds of wood here. And they're all good bow-building wood. You just need to find a piece you like, and we'll turn that stick into a bow.

I didn't know how I would decide. There must have been a hundred or more pieces of wood to look at. And I wanted to make the right choice. I wanted it to be as pretty as the bow he had originally given me.

"I don't know, Mr. Forrest," I said with a shrug on my shoulders. "I really liked the bow you gave me last night. What kind of wood was it made of?" I asked.

"Well, I told you that I made that bow for my son," Mr. Forrest began. "What I didn't tell you was the whole story behind it. You see, years ago, when my son learned about Indians—I think it was in the fourth grade— and found out there used to be Cherokees living all around where we live right now, he became fascinated with them. He read everything he could about the Cherokees—which, of course, meant I learned some things about them, too, because he was always telling me what he was learning. Well, one of the things we learned about the Cherokees is that they liked to build their bows from Black Locust trees. It's an excellent wood for building bows, and we still have a lot around here. And that's what I built his bow out of—Black Locust. He insisted upon it."

"Well..." I began with an unsure grin, "Can I insist upon it too?"

"You sure can," he said, giving me a pat on the shoulder before walking over to the staves and pulling a piece out. "This is a Black Locust stave," he explained as he handed it to me. "Is this what you want?" he looked at me and asked.

"Yes, sir," I answered. "If that's what the other bow was made with, it's what I want. I want it to look just like that one. We learned about Indians this year, too. And the Cherokees were my favorite, as well. So, it'd be cool to have a bow made out of the same wood they used to use. I didn't know any-thing about that."

"Alright, then. Sounds like it's time to get to work," Mr. Forrest said with a nod. "It's time to turn you into a bowyer."

# Chapter 17

"A bowyer? What's that?" I asked Mr. Forrest with a confused look on my face.

"Well, Parker, a bowyer is someone who makes bows. It's what I have been my whole life. And you're about to become one as well," he answered.

With that, he picked up the Black Locust stave and nodded for me to follow him, saying, "Let's head over to my bowyer's bench and get the bark off this tree."

The bowyer's bench was an old piece of wooden equipment Mr. Forrest said he made over forty years ago. It was long, like a bench in a baseball dugout. But you don't sit on it like you sit on a normal bench. Instead, you sit on one end of it, straddling it like you're riding a horse. And the stave lays down in front of you on the rest of the bench. There is also a big wooden arm above the bench that comes down and holds the stave in place. You bring the arm up and down using a footrest. When you press on the footrest, the arm comes down. When you take pressure off the footrest, the arm lifts back up. This is used to hold the stave in place so that you can work on it without it slipping and sliding around.

"Alright, son, the first thing we need to do is get this bow cut down to something that will fit you better than that last bow. I'm thinking fifty-four inches—which is about six inches shorter than that other bow. That should be just about right for you," Mr. Forrest explained.

He then grabbed a tape measure and a pencil, and I watched him mark off a line fifty-four inches from one end of the wood. He then took a hand saw and cut off the end of the stave right at the mark he had made, adding, "Yes, sir. That looks about right."

"Alright," he continued, "the next thing we have to do is get the bark off. And to do that, we use this," Mr. Forrest said as he held up an odd-looking tool I had never seen before. "It's called a draw knife," he explained. "And the reason it's called a draw knife is because you reach way out and lay it on the wood sitting out in front of you. Then you pull it, or draw it, back toward you." He said this while going through the motions.

Then, while sitting down at the bench and holding the stave in place using the footrest, he reached out and slowly pulled the blade across the wood, back toward himself. When he did, a long strip of bark came off with it. He then leaned back out over the stave, and while keeping pressure on the footrest so that the wooden arm held the piece of black locust firmly in place, he re-peated the process—lifting and removing another strip of bark. After that, he lifted his foot from the rest, which released the stave from the wooden arm's grip, and he rotated the stave so that another section of bark was facing upward. He then leaned back out over it and carefully pulled the draw knife all the way to himself once again, removing another long strip of bark.

"You see how that works?" he looked at me and asked.

"Yes, sir. That's pretty cool," I answered.

"You wanna give it a try," he asked, tip-ping his head down to look at me over his glasses.

"Ummm…. sure," I said hesitantly. "I'll give it a shot."

Mr. Forrest helped me get in place on the bench and guided me through everything he had just done. On my first try, I didn't pull off a full strip of bark like he had done. It was a little hard for me to hold down pressure on the footrest while pulling carefully with my arms. But, after a few tries and with a little more instruction from Mr. Forrest, I was doing pretty good.

"Ain't nothin' to it, is there?" he asked. "You're going to make a fine bowyer, indeed. Yes, siree, you've got this figured out, boy."

Once all the bark was removed from the stave, Mr. Forrest bumped me on the leg, indicating that he wanted me to take my foot off the footrest so that the bench's arm would let go of the stave. He picked up the now bare piece of wood and looked it over for a minute or two before saying, "This is a fine piece of wood, Parker. It's going to make a really good bow. One of the reasons the Cherokees picked these Black Locust trees for their bows is because they grew so straight compared to a lot of other trees. And this here was a good one, indeed. Nice and straight. Nice and straight," he added while continuing to look it over.

After placing the stave back on the bench, he said, "Okay, now it's time to pop a line."

I didn't know what he was talking about, but that didn't stop me from nodding like I did. I watched as Mr. Forrest pulled something out of his tool belt and began to stretch a string out from the device from one end of the stave to the other—long ways. There was some kind of blue powder on the string that was making a bit of a mess.

When he had the string stretched tightly from one end to the other, he said, "You wanna pop it?" I looked at him with a face that told him I didn't know what he meant. So, he said, "Grab the string right in the middle—just pinch it with a finger and your thumb—slowly raise it up until it's tight, and then let it go. You can't mess it up." I followed his instructions, and after the cloud of blue smoke disappeared, there was a nice blue line where the string had come down hard on the wood. It ran from one end of the stave to the other.

"Alright, now we have us a chalk line running right down the center of this stave. That line is going to be the center of your bow," he explained.

Then, after taking a pencil and a ruler and making several other marks on the wood, he grabbed my left hand and placed it right in the center of the stave, moving my fingers right where he wanted them, and drew some lines around my hand—where the grip would be. When he was done, he gave me a nod, and after I lifted my hand and looked at him to discover what was next, he said, "Well, all we have to do now is remove everything that isn't a bow."

And with that, he smiled and said, "But first, let's take a break."

# Chapter 18

Over the next few afternoons, Mr. Forrest showed me how to use other tools to slowly and carefully remove all the wood that was outside of the lines he had drawn on the stave that first day. The main tool we used was called a rasp, which is also apparently used when putting shoes on horses. It looks sort of like the files my mother and sister use on their nails—just bigger. It had one side that removes a lot of wood when you pull it across a stave and another side that removes less. I pushed and pulled on it for hours and hours as Mr. Forrest watched and gave me instructions—lending his help now and then when there were tough spots in the wood, like knots.

But, after just a few days of work, we had done what Mr. Forrest said we had to do. We removed everything from the stave that wasn't a bow—which meant we had a bow.

After giving me my first lesson in building a bowstring, he showed me how to use another tool called a stringer to put the string in place on the bow. "Using a stringer is much safer than bending the bow over your leg like you have seen me do. Remember, I've got a lot of practice. But I've also seen a lot of bows messed up that way by people who didn't know what they were doing. So always use a stringer," he added.

Now, with the bow strung, he passed it to me. It was not only beautiful, just like the first bow he gave me, but it also fit me perfectly. Mr. Forrest was definitely right about the shorter limbs and the smaller grip. This bow was just my size. And not only that, I was mostly excited to see that I could easily pull it back—and not just halfway, but all the way.

"Can we shoot it?" I pleaded.

"Not yet, son. We still need to put the finishing touches on it. But you'll be able to shoot it tomorrow. I promise," he said apologetically.

We spent the rest of that afternoon putting some wood stain and sealant on the bow. Doing that made it even more beautiful "and more durable too," Mr. Forrest explained. "That stain and sealant will keep moisture out of it. That bow will last you forever," he promised, "if you take care of it. But I know you will because you've put so much hard work into it."

"Yes, sir. I will. I promise I will," I agreed.

"Just one more thing to do, and we'll be done for the night," Mr. Forrest said as he walked over to a cabinet and began looking through it. "We need to add a grip. And this here will be perfect."

He was holding up some piece of material as he walked back toward me, but I wasn't sure what it was. It was scaly and weird-looking—kind of like a snakeskin but also like a piece of leather, and yet not exactly like either of them. "Do you know what this is?" he asked, answering before I could finish shaking my head no, "It's a beaver tail."

"Really?" I asked, pretty surprised as he passed it to me.

"That's right," he said. "And they make great grips on traditional bows. Let's get this one trimmed up and threaded in place on yours."

After doing some more measuring and using a needle and some thick string to secure the beaver tail firmly in place on the grip of my new bow, he handed it back to me, quickly saying, "Don't touch the finish.

The stain isn't completely dry yet. But it will be tomorrow. And tomorrow is Saturday, so you can shoot it all day if you want—assuming that your parents are okay with it."

I was sort of listening but mostly just looking. I couldn't believe we had built this bow and built it from scratch—from nothing but a piece of wood. And it was perfect. More beautiful even than the first bow he had given me. It fit me perfectly, and I could draw it back! Which meant I could shoot it. And yes, I did plan on shooting it all day on Saturday. There was nothing more that I wanted to do.

# Chapter 19

The next morning, I was up bright and early—earlier, even, than I had to get up on school mornings. I was too excited to sleep! I was ready to shoot my bow. Thankfully, my dad was ready for me to shoot it, too.

He had sort of been following along each day as Mr. Forrest and I built the bow, but when we showed it to him last night—completely finished—I could tell he was surprised at how well it turned out.

"How much of this did you do, and how much did Parker do?" my dad asked Mr. Forrest. "Oh, I'm guessing Parker did 75% of the work," he answered. "I showed him what to do and helped along the way, but he did most of it himself. And let me warn you, you better watch out, or he'll be the bowyer around here and not you," Mr. Forrest finished with a smile.

"Well, I'm proud of you, Parker," my dad said as he patted me on the back. "And I am proud for this to be the first bow made in our new shop—the first Sticks and Strings bow ever built."

I hadn't thought about that. But it was pretty cool that I had built the first bow in our family's new business.

"But it better be the first of many," he added, "because the bills are piling up, and they are piling up fast."

———

When Dad and I got to the shop on Saturday morning, Mr. Forrest was already there. He was over at his bench finishing up some arrows.

"What are these for?" I asked, leaning over the workbench.

"Well, hey there, Parker. They're for you," he answered.

"For me?" I asked, certain he was playing—because these arrows had big, bright pink feathers on them. "I don't want pink arrows," I protested. "No way!"

"Well, whether you want them or not, that's what you're getting," Mr. Forrest answered. "I've got some reasons for it, and you'll just have to trust me."

"But…" I began, continuing my protest, only to be shut down by Mr. Forrest's raised hand.

"You want me to teach you to shoot, right?" Mr. Forrest asked. "We didn't build that bow just so you could look at it, did we? No sir. You want to learn how to shoot it, and more importantly, you want to learn how to hunt with it, don't you?"

I nodded in agreement without saying anything else. But no matter what I wanted, I didn't want arrows that looked like they were my sister's.

"Well," Mr. Forrest continued, "if you want me to teach you how to shoot this bow, you are going to have to do things my way. Okay? And sometimes you are just going to have to trust me, even when you don't understand. I've been doing this a long time, and I promise you there's a reason for those pink feathers."

I couldn't imagine what that reason would be. But again, at this point, I just wanted to shoot my bow. So, I gave in, saying, "Okay. They're fine, then. I'm just ready to shoot it no matter what color the feathers are."

"Alright, then. Let's get going," Mr. Forrest said, obviously pleased with my change of heart. Then I watched as he gathered up about six of the arrows and nodded for me to grab my bow.

I walked over to the workbench where we had left my bow to dry the night before and asked, "Is it okay to touch it?"

"Yes, it's completely dry," he answered as he walked toward the shooting range we had set up in the back of the shop. "I checked it this morning, and it's ready to go."

So, I placed my hand on the beaver tail grip and lifted the bow off the bench, admiring its beauty and noticing again how well it fit into my hand. I still couldn't believe we had made it.

As I approached Mr. Forrest, who was standing over at the shooting range, he began his instruction. "Alright, before you'll be ready to go after deer with this bow, you are going to have to be able to put arrow after arrow in a circle about like this," he explained as he lifted up his hands in front of his face, holding them in the shape of a circle a little smaller than a basketball. "About the size of a paper plate is what we're after. Preferably a small paper plate."

"But there are two parts to that—two parts to aiming," he continued. "First, there's the left and right part of the aiming—or the windage. Second, there's the up and down part—or the elevation. And we are going to learn those two parts separately," he explained while making sure from the nod of my head that I was following along.

I had already begun wondering about the aiming part because I had noticed that both the bow he gave me the first day I met him and also the one we just built—neither of those bows had sights. When I shot Mason's bow—his compound bow—it had a little circle back on the string that you peeked through with your eye and little pins up front that you put on the target. You'd pick a different pin depending on how far away from the target you were. But these traditional bows didn't have either of those things. No little circle on the string—which Mason said was called a peep sight—and no pins up front.

So, when I got the chance, I politely interrupted Mr. Forrest and asked, "But how do you aim if there aren't any sights? On the compound bow I shot, there was a way to aim. But on this bow, there's nothing like that."

"I figured you were wondering about that," Mr. Forrest answered. "Because everyone who's ever shot a compound bow and moves to a traditional bow does. But let me explain it like this, Parker. You're a baseball player, right? Your dad says you're a pretty good one, probably the best pitcher in your league."

I was kind of embarrassed to hear him say that, but I nodded in agreement. I loved baseball and really was good at it.

"Well," Mr. Forrest continued, "when you walk up on that pitcher's mound, and you need to put that ball right into the dead center of the catcher's mitt, what do you do? Do you have any sights to use? Any peep sight to look through or any pins sitting out in front of you?"

That made me smile because I could kind of see where he was going. "No sir," I answered, "I just look really hard at where I want the ball to go…"

"And you just rear back and throw it, don't you?" Mr. Forrest jumped back in, getting sort of excited. "You don't need no sights to throw a baseball, and you don't need no sights to shoot a bow. You just need to practice. You need to practice it over and over and over again until it just becomes natural to you—like throwing a baseball. Does that make sense?"

"I guess so," I said with a nod. It really did make sense when he said it that way.

"So that's what we're going to be doing over the next several weeks and months," he continued. "We are going to be practicing every day until your body just knows what to do when you pull back on that string and look at where you want the arrow to go. Again, just like when you throw a baseball."

By this time, I was past ready to shoot, so I nodded again in agreement.

"But to begin," he continued, "we are going to start out by only worrying about the first part of aiming—just the left and right, or the windage—for right now. We ain't worryin' today or tomorrow, or even next week about the up and down part of aiming. Just the left and right for now, okay?"

I didn't really understand why we'd be doing it this way. But I wasn't going to push back like I had done with the pink feathers. So, I said, "Yes, sir. I've got it." Again, I just really wanted to shoot.

# Chapter 20

So, once I showed him I understood, Mr. Forrest walked down to the target and turned it around. The backside of it was solid black—with no circles or bullseyes to aim for, like on the front. Then, after turning the target around, he pulled off a long strip of white duct tape from the roll he was carrying in his hand, and he ran it right down the center of the target, from top to bottom, before turning around and walking back to me.

"Alright, Parker," he said when he made it back, "all I am worried about right now is you hitting or getting close to hitting that strip of duct tape with your arrow. I don't care whether it's in the middle of the target, at the top of the target, or at the bottom of the target. I just want you to hit or get close to that duct tape with your arrow. Got it?"

"Got it," I confirmed.

"But, to do that consistently, time and time again," he continued, "you have to draw and anchor your bow back consistently, time and time again. You can't draw it back one way one time and then draw it back another way another time and expect your arrow to land in the same place. Make sense?" he asked.

"Yes, sir. That makes complete sense," I agreed.

"Okay," he continued, "there are a couple of ways to grab the string and draw the bow. But I am going to teach you to do it the way I do it. It's the split-finger method. And what I mean by split-finger is that once you place the arrow on the string, you are going to place your pointer finger above the arrow's nock and your middle finger just below it—which means those two fingers are split apart just enough for the arrow nock to sit between them," Mr. Forrest explained while holding his hand up and demonstrating it to me. "Then," he kept going, "you'll use your pointer finger, your middle finger, and your ring finger to pull back on the string. Does that make sense?" he asked, looking at me to see if it did.

I nodded to show that I was following along.

"And so, when you pull the bowstring back to your face," Mr. Forrest continued, "I want you to pull it back right to where your middle finger touches the corner of your mouth. You might even want to use that pointy tooth—the upper one—because it never moves. Just touch the tip of your finger to the tip of your tooth." He smiled and pointed at the tooth he was talking about.

"And then, you should also be able to rest the base of your thumb at the back of your jaw. There's like a little nook back there it will slide into once you get used to it."

Then, after grabbing my bow and demonstrating the whole process to me, he handed it back and said, "Okay, are you ready to give it a try?"

*I was ready when I got here an hour ago,* I thought to myself. But only answered by saying, "Yes, sir. Let's do it."

"Alright, put this glove on. It will keep your fingers from getting sore. And let's start at ten yards—and again, don't worry about the up and down for now. Just work on drawing back to the same spot on your face, which means your eyes will be lined up in the same way with your arrow every time. And do your best to hit that strip of tape. That's all we are worried about right now— just the left and right part of aiming."

And with that, he handed me an arrow and watched as I struggled to nock it on the string with the new leather glove on my hand. Then, after telling me to draw slowly, Mr. Forrest stood beside me, watching my every move. Once the string was nearly all the way back, he said, "Hit your anchor points—the corner of your mouth and back behind your jaw. And look hard at the center of that strip of white tape. I mean, stare a hole through it."

After doing everything he said, I relaxed my fingers and let the string slip quickly away from my glove. But before I could move, Mr. Forrest was saying, "Hold up. Hold up. Don't move. I forgot to tell you this. But when you release the string, don't move a muscle until you hear the arrow hit the target. Go ahead and take a look, though. Not bad for your first shot."

When I looked, the arrow had hit the target pretty high, but just slightly to the right of the tape.

"So, what do you need to do?" he looked at me and asked.

It was pretty obvious. "I need to bring it down and to the left," I answered.

"No," he responded quickly. "What did I say? We ain't worryin' about the up and down right now," he said with a smile. "So, you just need to bring it to the left."

"Oh yeah… just to the left," I agreed, still not understanding why we weren't worried about the up and down.

———————

The next several shots after that first one got better and better. With about half of them hitting somewhere on the tape. Mr. Forrest was pretty excited about it, and I was too. But then, after about fifteen to twenty minutes of shooting, I was starting to get

tired. And after I missed the target alto-
gether for the second time in three shots, Mr.
Forrest said, "Looks like you need a break,
son. Let's grab us something to drink and sit
down for a bit."

"But I'm not tired!" I insisted with a lot
of frustration in my voice. "I don't need to
rest. My arms aren't worn out at all." I was
super irritated that I had started missing so
badly. Not to mention that when I missed
the target the second time, my arrow
skipped across the concrete floor, making a
loud noise, and my dad jokingly yelled,
"Don't let him tear up the shop, Forrest."
They both thought it was funny. I didn't.

"I didn't say that your arms were tired,
son. What's tired is your brain," Mr. Forrest
answered. "It's hard to maintain the level of
focus you have to have to shoot a bow for
longer than fifteen or twenty minutes at a
time. Let's go rest your brain for a bit, and
we'll get back to it. Plus, if we don't take a

break, your arms will be tired soon enough. And then you'll start shooting bad for sure."

I still wasn't convinced.

# Chapter 21

We practiced on and off the rest of the morning. There were a lot of ups and downs—and I'm not talking about aiming or where the arrow was hitting. (Remember, Mr. Forrest wouldn't let me worry about that yet—even though I was.) But I'm talking about shooting good for a while and shooting bad for a while. Or shooting good one shot and bad the next shot. And then missing the target completely a whole lot more. It was horrible. And my mood was getting horrible, too.

Mr. Forrest could always tell me what I had done wrong when I missed. Usually, it had something to do with me not getting my finger anchored to the corner of my mouth or with me not releasing the bowstring smoothly enough. But no matter what was going on, I was frustrated. In fact, I got so frustrated that, eventually, Mr. Forrest had to say that it was enough for the day.

"Parker, you're too frustrated now to shoot any good. But I want you to listen to me here and trust me when I say: you ain't the first person to get there with one of these bows. That's why a lot of folks call them struggle sticks," he laughed, probably hoping I would too. But I didn't.

"Because," he continued, "it sure can be a struggle to shoot them well. It takes a lot of time and a lot of practice. And son, you've only been at it for a few hours. So, you can't let yourself get frustrated about it so quickly. You'll figure it out soon enough. Your brain will figure it out soon enough. That's what it's all about, really. Doing it enough times that your brain has the chance to start putting your hands where they need to be so that the arrow hits where you're looking."

But no matter what he said, I was certain that I was terrible. I was just as certain that I wouldn't get any better. There was no way I was killing a deer with one of these bows. I could barely hit the target at ten yards. And I don't know anyone who's killed a deer at ten yards! This whole thing was going to be impossible. I was certain of it.

And so, after his little pep talk, I didn't say a word. The truth was, I was ready to give up. So, I just turned around from Mr. Forrest, walked back to the workbench, and sat my bow down right back in the spot from where I had picked it up earlier that morning. I then walked to my dad's office, called my mom, and begged her to come get me.

———————

"What's wrong, honey?" Mom asked as I stepped into the van. "Why are you upset?"

131

I didn't feel like answering, so I didn't.

She left it alone for a while, but after a few more minutes, she asked, "Is something wrong with your bow? I don't know what it could be. Your dad told me last night that it looked amazing. Did you get to shoot it today?"

"Yes, Mom!" I finally blurted out. "I got to shoot it, and it was terrible—I was terrible. I mean, I shot okay for a little while. But then it got to where I could hardly hit the target. And I was only shooting from ten yards! There's no way I could ever kill a deer shooting like that!"

"Well, no, honey, you probably couldn't. But you also couldn't have struck out a single batter the first time you tried to pitch this year. In fact, the only thing I remember about that first practice where you tried was you *pitching a fit*—sort of like you are now. But I also remember that in your last game of the season, you struck out almost everyone and almost pitched a no-hitter. So, what do you think the difference was on that first night versus that last night?"

I didn't answer.

"Parker, answer me," she demanded. "What was the difference?"

Of course, I knew the answer. It was practice. But I still didn't answer. So, she continued on.

"You're way too hard on yourself, son. You expect to be the best at everything you do right from the beginning. But that's not how the world works. If you are going to be good at anything, you have to work at it. And if you get frustrated and give up the first time you try something and find out it's hard, you won't ever be able to get good at anything, which is sad because one thing your father and I both know about you is that you can be good at pretty much anything you set your mind to. God has given you a lot of talent—athletic and otherwise. But for you to make the most of that, you've got to be more patient with yourself. And you've got to be willing to put in the work it takes to become as good as you can be."

I knew she was right. She knew me better than I knew myself. I did always want to be the best at everything I tried—right from the start. My dad is the same way. He had told me before that is why he didn't play golf. "That, plus it's boring," he once laughed. But he admitted, "When I wasn't immediately as good at it as I was at other sports, I wasn't interested, so I quit playing." Which I knew was exactly what I was trying to do with archery. So, I fessed up.

"You're right, Mom," I quietly admitted. "I have a hard time when I'm not the best at something right away. And I guess it feels easier to just give up—especially when you know there is something else you could do. When I was in there today with Mr. Forrest, struggling like I was, all I could do was think about how much better I shot Mason's bow. And I was shooting that day from 20 yards or more. But there I was this morning, and after about fifteen minutes, I could hardly hit the target—not even from ten yards. And so, I was ready to give up. I still am, kind of."

"But you can't, Parker," my mom insisted. "I have no doubt you can be as good at this as you are at baseball—if you'll practice. In fact, when I asked your dad last night how he thought your practice would go today, he said, 'I don't know how it will go on his first day, but shooting a traditional bow is a whole lot like throwing a baseball—it's mostly hand/eye coordination—and one thing we both know for sure about Parker, he's got more of that than most people walking around on the planet. He'll be fine if he's patient enough to stick with it."

I guess my dad knew me better than I knew myself, too.

# Chapter 22

We were only five minutes from the house when we finished talking, but I knew what I had to say. So, I did. "Take me back, Mom."

"Huh," she looked into the rearview mirror and asked.

"I'm sorry I called you. But I need to go back. I can't quit," I answered, watching her expression in the mirror change to a smile.

"Okay, then. How about some lunch first?" she answered.

---

After the talk with my mom that afternoon, I made up my mind that I wasn't going to give up so quickly just because it had been tougher than I thought. It was called a struggle stick for a reason, but I was now determined to win the struggle. And so, when I got back to Sticks and Strings and found my dad and Mr. Forrest having their lunch, I walked into the break area to apologize. And I didn't beat around the bush.

"I'm sorry I acted like a baby earlier today," I began. "When I started missing the target, I got frustrated. I guess I thought it would be easy and that I would be good right from the start. I'm sorry I left like that."

"Parker," Mr. Forrest looked at me and said, "I don't think you acted like a baby. You only acted like most kids your age do when they find that shooting a traditional bow is harder than it looks. I've even seen some grown men act like that when the ol' struggle stick got the best of them. And for you to walk in here and apologize like you did, and for you to have the guts to come back like you've done, tells me you're more of a man than most."

I saw my dad nodding in agreement before he said, "That's the truth, son. Storming out of here mad wasn't the right thing to do, but coming back and apologizing was—and more than makes up for it. So, I say we just pretend like it never happened and move on. How does that sound?"

Of course, that sounded good to me. It did to Mr. Forrest, too. And so, after he gobbled up the last few bites of his sandwich, he looked at me and said, "Are you ready to get back at it?"

"I was born ready," I answered with a confident smile.

"Yes, you were," he replied. "Yes, you were."

———

"For the rest of the afternoon, we are going to shoot one arrow at a time," Mr. Forrest explained as we were walking back toward the

139

shooting range. That will help keep you from getting tired, and it will give you a chance to think about things between each shot. And," he continued, "we've got other work to do around here besides shooting. Your dad can't do it all. So, for the remainder of the day, we'll spend half of each hour shooting and the other half getting some things done that we need to get done if we are going to start selling some bows. How does that sound?"

"Sounds good," I answered as he handed me an arrow.

———————

For the rest of the afternoon, we'd shoot for about fifteen minutes and then set the bow down to continue getting the shop in order. And by the time my dad and I turned off the lights that afternoon, locking the door behind us, everything was looking much better—the shop, my shooting, and my attitude.

"This is pretty exciting, isn't it?" he asked as we were driving home. "Certainly not anything I would have expected even a month ago. Who would have ever thought we'd own an archery business?"

"Not me," I leaned forward and answered. "And who would have ever thought that I would have built my own bow?"

"Well, you had some good help, for sure," he answered. "That Mr. Forrest is something else, isn't he? And I really believe that if you keep listening to him and doing exactly what he says, you'll be deadly accurate with that bow before you know it."

I believed that, too. But I was about to find out how hard listening to Mr. Forrest and doing exactly what he said was really going to be.

# Chapter 23

For the next week, all I did was shoot at the line of tape on the target. I mean, we did some other things around the shop, too, but nothing changed about the archery practice—day after day after day. And just when I thought I couldn't stand it anymore, Mr. Forrest promised me on Friday afternoon that starting next week, we'd mix it up a bit. "You're doing great, Parker—much better than you should be after just a week. But we're going to take a break this weekend, okay? Your body needs some time to rest, and your brain needs some time to absorb and process everything you've learned this week."

I didn't hear much after he said we were going to do something new next week. I was certainly done with what we had been doing and was ready for something else. I expected that it was time to start worrying about the up and down part of the aiming, too.

But I'd find out on Monday that I was wrong.

––––––––––

"Alright, Parker," Mr. Forrest said as I made my way back to his workbench on Monday morning. "You ready to mix things up a bit?"

"Yes, sir," I answered. "More than you know," I continued with a smile. "Shooting at that line of tape was starting to get boring."

"Well, I hope you're not too bored with it. Because you've got a lot more of it to do.

But today, we'll start practicing it from fifteen yards, too. In fact, I just marked off a new line for you at that distance," he said while pointing over to a new line on the floor of the shooting range.

*Wait. This is what he meant by mixing it up? You've got to be kidding me! I can't keep doing this.* My brain could hardly handle the thought of it. But I had promised I would do exactly what he said, so I went along with it. For a few days at least.

But by Friday afternoon, I couldn't stand it anymore. I was seeing that stupid line of white duct tape in my sleep! In fact, I think we had gone through a whole roll of it in the two weeks I'd been shooting at it. I was now hitting it or nearly hitting it with just about every arrow. If I missed by more than a few inches, from either ten or fifteen yards, I knew it was time for a break, and I'd take one. During those breaks, there was still a lot to do around the shop, and Mr. Forrest was already working on our first bow order from my dad's old boss. So, I'd walk over and watch as he taught Dad to do the same things he'd taught me when we built my bow.

But, when they finished that bow on Friday, and Mr. Forrest asked me if I was ready for another practice session, I just shook my head from side to side and said, "No. I'm kind of tired."

"Alright," he answered. "Are you sure that's it? Or is there something else going on?"

*Something else other than I'm TIRED of doing the same old thing, day after day?* I thought to myself. But I didn't want to say that out loud. And yet, I was really wanting to start shooting at something other than a vertical line. I was ready to start working on something else. So, I said it.

"I guess there is something else," I began. "I'm ready to work on something new.

When can I start practicing something other than shooting at that stupid piece of tape? I'm so tired of it. We've been doing it for two weeks. I'm ready to start working on the up and down part," I insisted.

"You're almost ready," Mr. Forrest answered calmly. "You're almost there. But not quite. Again, Parker, you're just going to have to trust that I know what I'm doing. Plus, what's the rush? It's not even July yet. We'll get you where you want to be before school starts back, I promise."

"Before school starts back?" I complained. "That's how long it's going to take?"

"Actually, it's going to take longer than that," he answered. "If you want to get good at traditional archery and stay good at it, you'll have to practice hard for the rest of your life."

"But when am I going to be ready for the next step?" I demanded. "I'm tired of shooting at that stupid line of tape from ten yards and then fifteen yards and then from ten yards again," I continued complaining.

"Well, you'll be happy to know that next week, you'll get to work on it from twenty yards, too," he said without a hint of a smile.

"Ugh!" I huffed out as I turned away from him and walked over to the bench, where I sat down my bow—more than ready to be done for the day.

"See you on Monday," Mr. Forrest said, as I stormed away.

# Chapter 24

"Dad," I complained on the way home, "I can't do this anymore. It's just the same old stuff. I'm not learning anything new. He hasn't taught me one new thing in two weeks!"

"I bet you're learning more than you realize, son. Mr. Forrest knows what he's doing. I can't believe everything he taught me this week about building bows. Your sister ought to have the website going by next week, and hopefully, the orders will start coming in, and he can help me build some more."

"But Dad, what about me?" I interrupted. "What about my shooting? When is he going to teach me something new?"

"I guess when you're ready, Parker," he answered without really telling me anything. "You've just got to trust him. He knows what he's doing. And you will too by the time he's done with you."

---

But on Monday, it was just more of the same. Yes, I was now mixing in shots from twenty yards, too. But I was still shooting a single arrow at a time at that stupid line of tape. While it was definitely harder at first, by Tuesday, it wasn't much harder than doing it from the closer distances—a little, but not much. Regardless, I wasn't sure how much longer I could do it. In fact, I was about ready to quit again. And by the time Wednesday afternoon rolled around—after another full day of shooting at that line, I had had enough.

"This is stupid," I blurted out. "I can't do this anymore. Shooting at this stupid line of tape has nothing to do with killing a deer. I don't even understand what the purpose is. I'm done," I finished as I walked over and sat the bow down.

"Stupid, huh?" Mr. Forrest answered without moving from where he had been standing on the shooting range. "I thought you wanted to learn to shoot that bow. When did doing that become stupid?" he asked.

"But I'm not learning to shoot the bow," I protested. "Not in a way that matters. Who shoots at a line of tape? At the least, I could shoot at a normal target. But for almost three weeks, I've been doing nothing but shooting at a line of tape. And it's pointless!" I added.

"Pointless?" Mr. Forrest said with a nod as he walked down to the target and spun it around—to the side with the bullseye. "Why don't you bring me that bow, and let's find out just how stupid and pointless all this practice has really been. Come on, get it," he insisted with a hand gesture that told me to hurry.

I wasn't sure what was about to happen. And was sort of regretting that I had spoken up. But I also watched him spin the target around and knew that meant something.

When I made it back over to him, he was standing at the ten-yard mark. He didn't say anything but just handed me an arrow and nodded toward the target.

I still didn't know what he wanted. I hadn't done this before. "Do I aim at the bullseye?" I asked hesitantly.

"Yes. Stare a hole through it and let the arrow go," he answered.

So, I drew the bow back, making sure to anchor on my tooth and my jaw, and once there, I took a second or so to stare hard at the center of the red bullseye on the target. Almost without knowing it, the arrow slipped from my hand, and when I heard that familiar THWACK sound made by the arrow hitting the target, I lowered the bow and saw my arrow in the smack dead center of the bullseye.

My mouth dropped wide open in disbelief. Mr. Forrest only handed me another arrow before saying, "Do it again."

So, I took the arrow and nocked it on my string. I placed my three gloved fingers around it and drew back to my face, making sure to hit my two anchor points. Then, after staring a hole through the bullseye once again—the bullseye that now had an actual hole in it from my first arrow—I relaxed my fingers and let the second arrow go. It landed on the target with another loud THWACK, and I couldn't believe it when it, too, was sitting right next to the first arrow in the center of the bullseye.

"Do it again," Mr. Forrest said as he handed me a third arrow.

Once again, the results were the same. I had put three arrows in the bullseye, so close that the feathers were all touching. But I didn't know how. I had never even practiced anything other than shooting at the vertical line of tape.

"Stupid, huh? Sort of like those pink feathers," Mr. Forrest said with a grin and a laugh.

"What in the world just happened?" I looked at him and asked.

"Practice. That's what happened."

"But I never practiced the up and down," I reminded him.

"No. That's where you're wrong, Parker," he corrected me. "You've been practicing it since the first day we got started—you just didn't know it. There's a reason I put those pink feathers on your arrows. It was so that your eyes could better follow them as they made their way from your bow to the target. While you didn't know you were paying attention to that, you were. And the whole time, your brain was taking notes. It was learning how the arrow flew, and so when you aimed at that bullseye just now, it was ready and knew just what to do. When you looked at the bullseye, your brain made the calculations and knew exactly where to place your bow to put the arrow in the dead center of the target. Again, sort of like throwing a baseball."

"I think pink is my new favorite color!" I joked.

"Well, if you keep these pink feathers in the woods, it'll pay dividends for you there, too," Mr. Forrest replied. "They really stand out in the shadows, and it helps you to see exactly where you hit the deer."

Mr. Forrest really knew what he was doing—even more than I first realized.

"So, what's next?" I asked.

"Oh, not much, Parker," he answered with a smile. "Just more practice. A lot more practice."

# Chapter 25

For the rest of the summer, I joined my dad and Mr. Forrest at the shop every day. My sister had the website and the social media stuff up and running, and we were beginning to make some sales—but "not nearly enough," my dad continued to worry.

My mom was there every day, working hard, too. She handled the business side of things while Dad and Mr. Forrest built bows. Dad was getting really good at building them, and I was getting really good at shooting them. Because while I helped out around the bow shop when and where I could, I spent most of my time on the shooting range, sending arrow after arrow into the target. And so, by the time school started back, I was good—real good. And, as always, whenever school started back, me and the rest of the Hunt Club Kids began to think about our favorite subject—hunting.

"So, are you ready to hunt with that new bow?" Mason asked as we were walking in together one morning, just a few days after school started back up.

"I sure am. I've worked hard all summer to get good at it. And from anywhere between ten to twenty yards, I'm pretty deadly," I answered.

"Are you going to get to practice out any further than that before the season starts?" Mason replied. "It's pretty tough to get a deer inside twenty yards."

"Yeah, I guess I'll need to," I answered. "Twenty yards is pretty close. But I'm sure we'll start working on that soon. Mr. Forrest knows what he's doing," I assured both of us.

---

Our new afternoon routine included Mom or Dad picking up Piper and me from school and taking us to Sticks and Strings, where we'd help out for the rest of the day. In a few months, Piper would have her driver's license, and according to my parents, "She'd become the bus driver." But for now, one of them would pick us up each day.

When I got to the shop on the day after Mason and I had talked about shooting out past twenty yards, I came in wanting to ask Mr. Forrest about it. He and Dad were both standing around the printer, trying to figure out how to make it work, when my mom, my sister, and I walked in.

Mom walked over and touched a button, and an order for two bows came out. That got us all excited, and Dad, Mr. Forrest, and

I walked out of the office area to start picking out the wood we'd need to build them.

As we were walking, I asked Mr. Forrest about practicing at distances past twenty yards. His response really surprised me.

"Ain't no need for that, son. We don't shoot past twenty yards with these bows. Too much can go wrong when you do," he explained.

"Huh? Really? Well, how in the world will we ever kill anything? How will we get a shot?" I replied, worried and confused.

"What do you mean?" he asked. "We just wait until a deer comes inside twenty yards, and then we take the shot."

"But does that ever happen?" I asked. "I mean, twenty yards is close, isn't it?"

"Well, son, not to toot my own horn, but I've put over two hundred deer in my freezer who all did. In fact, most of them were way closer than that when I shot them."

"But how? How do you get them that close?" I replied, desperately wanting to know the answer.

"Well, son," he continued as my dad began to look through a few of the staves he had pulled out for the new bows, "that's what we'll be working on next. Hunting season is right around the corner, which means class is about to be in session again."

"Good," I answered. "Because if I am going to get one with my bow this year, I still have a lot to learn. I can't even begin to imagine..." And that's when Dad cut me off.

"Parker," he turned away from the staves and interrupted me, saying, "Buddy, you aren't going to be hunting with that bow this year."

"Well, which one will I be hunting with?" I asked back, pretty confused now. "I don't have another one."

"No, son," he answered. "Mr. Forrest and I have talked, and we both feel like you need to wait another year—at least until you're twelve. Which fortunately, with your birthday being in September, that's how old you'll be when bow season starts next October.

"But I don't want to wait until next October, Dad!" I complained loudly. "I've been practicing all summer, working hard to get ready for this deer season. I know I'm ready. I'll be eleven next month, and I know I'm ready. Tell him, Mr. Forrest!" I turned to him and pleaded.

"Parker," Mr. Forrest answered, "you're shooting that bow just fine—better than fine, in fact. But it's one thing to do that in here, and a whole other thing to do it in the woods when you're eye to eye with a deer, and your heart is thumping out of your chest. So, I'm going to have to side with your dad on this one. I didn't let my son hunt with his bow until he was fourteen. So be thankful you're not going to have to wait that long."

# Chapter 26

Oh, I was furious.

"Why didn't either of you tell me this at the beginning of the summer?" I demanded. "Why have you let me practice all this time not knowing."

"Parker, I never thought you'd plan on hunting with that bow this year. You just built it a couple of months ago. I never thought for a minute you'd be ready to use it this season. And I guess I assumed you'd know that, too. But it looks like that was a mistake on my part. And I'm sorry, son. I guess we should have talked about it."

I tried to make my case for another minute or two, but I wasn't getting anywhere. They weren't budging.

"You'll still be getting to hunt, son. Both with me and Mr. Forrest," my dad said, trying to calm me down. "Like he was just saying, Mr. Forrest has a whole lot he wants to teach you this year—about how to hunt with these traditional bows."

"And the best place to teach you that is in the woods, chasing after deer," Mr. Forrest added. "And we'll still keep practicing with your bow—to make sure you're more than ready when you get your chance next year."

I still wasn't happy about the situation, but there wasn't any more use in arguing. Their minds were made up. Plus, there was still rifle season, which started in November and lasted into February. I knew I'd have plenty of opportunities then.

"Fine," I said, ready to put the argument to rest. "I'll still have plenty of time to hunt with my rifle anyway. I guess it's not that big of a deal."

When I said that, it was almost like I sucked the breath out of my dad's lungs. I saw it, and Mr. Forrest did, too. "Parker," Dad began to answer with his eyes still closed, "we are in the traditional bowhunting business now. And I mean fully committed to that and to nothing else. That's the only way we can do things now if we are going to be authentic about it. Which means there are no more rifle hunts for us. Traditional bowhunting is it, from here on out."

If my question had taken the air out of his lungs, his answer had certainly done the same to mine.

"So, I won't be hunting at all this year?" I asked, having put the pieces together in my head.

"You'll be hunting plenty, son," my dad began to answer. "Much more than you've been able to do over the past few years with me so busy flying all over the country. But you just won't be the one carrying the bow."

"Parker," Mr. Forrest said as he laid his hand on my shoulder.

I ran off before he could finish.

# Chapter 27

So far in my time hunting, I had only taken two deer—a nice doe when I was nine and a decent buck last season when I was ten. Even though we mounted that buck, the other Hunt Club Kids were far ahead of me when it came to deer hunting. I was hoping this would be the year I'd begin to catch up. But there was no chance of that now.

Mr. Forrest came and found where I was hiding. When he did, he sat down beside me and said, "I know you're upset at your dad—and probably at me too for agreeing with him. But we both believe this is for the best. We also both believe this is still going to be a great hunting season for you. If you approach it in the right way and with the right attitude, you'll learn a lot, and you'll be a real hunter come this time next year."

I didn't say anything back.

"Listen, I've got a lot to teach you about hunting in the old ways. Some people still do it the way I'm going to teach you, but not many. I promise you, though, by the time we're done with this season, you're going to know more about getting close to deer than any kid you know. I promise you that, Parker. But you have to get on board with it, okay?"

That sounded pretty good to me. But I was still mad. So, instead of saying anything, I just looked at him with a half smile and nodded. And with that, he said, "Come on, we've got work to do."

———

My dad, Mr. Forrest, and I spent the rest of the day beginning the work on the two new bows that had been ordered. When it was about time to go home, Dad looked at me and said, "You wanna shoot some before we leave?"

I certainly did, and I also wanted to see him shoot the new bow he had built for himself—with Mr. Forrest's help, of course. So, I said, "Yeah, let's make it a competition!"

"Alright, you're on!" my dad answered as he walked over and grabbed our bows. "Five rounds, one arrow each round. Mr. Forrest is the judge."

There's no better way to describe what happened than just saying it. I wore him out. I mean, it wasn't even close. Of course, after whipping his tail like that, I wanted to point out that it might make more sense for him to let me do the hunting this year, but Mr. Forrest beat me to it—even though they still weren't changing their minds.

Regardless, I left feeling better that night. And I couldn't help getting pretty excited about the start of hunting season, which was just a little more than a month and a half away now—even though I wouldn't get to carry my bow.

———————

The next day at school, I explained the situation to Wyatt, Jet, and Mason. They all made me feel better about it. And Mason even admitted that he was kind of jealous.

"I'll switch places with you if you want," he said. "I'd love for someone to show me how to get that close to a deer on a regular basis."

"Yeah, no kidding," Jet agreed. "My dad has been chasing deer with his traditional bow for a few years now, and well—he still is—just chasing them, I mean."

Of course, all of this made me feel better. Even though I was bummed a little to hear that the group hunt at Wyatt's house we had talked about back over the summer was going to be held on the Saturday of Alabama's Youth Weekend. I had killed my first deer on that Saturday two seasons ago, and I knew that the other boys would have a good chance of getting more deer for themselves this year.

"But," Wyatt was quick to add, "y'all are still welcome to come. Your dad can still bow hunt the property. Who knows, with that deer ninja, Mr. Forrest, teaching y'all what to do, you might show us all up."

"Ain't no doubt about that," Mason agreed.

And so that was the plan. But Youth Weekend was still a ways away, and me and Mr. Forrest had a lot of hunting to do between now and then.

# Chapter 28

Over the next six or seven weeks leading up to bow season, we focused mostly on the business. It seemed that business had picked up a bit, "likely because bow season was approaching, and people were wanting new bows," my dad had said. And the extra orders meant extra work—for all of us.

But that still left plenty of time for shooting in the evenings. And during a lot of that time, Mr. Forrest and I were able to talk about the many ways hunting with him this year would be different than the type of hunting I had done before. It was going to be way different and way harder than I thought—maybe even impossible.

"So, Mr. Forrest," I began to ask him one night, "you said a while back that you don't ever shoot past twenty yards, right?"

"Yep, that's right," he agreed. "I mean, I don't carry one of those fancy, dancy range finders with me. So, I guess I might shoot one every now and then at twenty-one or twenty-two yards. But, for the most part, I'd say I shoot them inside of fifteen, often inside of twelve or even ten," he continued.

"Wow. That's crazy," I answered. "So, you must use some really good camo, then. To be able to get that close to them."

"Hshh," he chuckled through his nostrils, "I ain't ever owned a lick of that stuff. That's not to say that it don't work," he continued, "nor that some of it ain't good. But I'm living proof that you ain't got to have it. Again, I'm not tooting my own horn here, but the two hundred or more deer that have taken a ride in the back of my truck over the years never saw me, and all I was wearing during most of those hunts was a plain ol' plaid shirt and some dark pants. Which is what you'll be wearing this year, too."

"So, you must climb up really high in your tree stands—so that they don't see you. How high do you go—more than twenty feet?" I asked.

"Only way I'm climbing a tree in the woods is if a bear is chasin' me," he laughed. "And that really ain't going to do much good either, seein' that they can climb better than I can. No, sir, I'm a ground hunter. Too scared of heights to climb a tree. But even if I wasn't, I don't see any good reason to do it. That's just chaining yourself to one spot. I like to be able to move and make adjustments depending on the wind and what I'm seeing, and so forth. No, I mostly hunt in two ways. I either still-hunt—which means moving through the woods very, very slowly, stopping now and then to be still for a bit. Or I go into a place where I know the deer are moving through and then tuck into some good natural cover. Then, I wait to ambush one when it walks by. I've killed some that walked within five yards of me while set up that way."

While I certainly didn't think that Mr. Forrest was stretching the truth, I did find all of this hard to believe. I had just never heard of anyone hunting like this. Most people bragged about how far away the deer was when they shot it, and Mr. Forrest seemed to be more proud when he shot one up close. This was just a totally different way of thinking for me. And I was still having a hard time believing it was even possible.

But bow season was starting next week, which meant I'd soon know for sure.

# Chapter 29

"Okay, Parker, follow me," Mr. Forrest whispered. "And walk as silently as you can. Remember, keep your weight on your back foot as you step forward, and search the ground with your other foot before you bring it down. You need to make sure there isn't anything under there that is going to crack when you put your weight on it."

I nodded without saying anything.

After a few weeks of getting all excited, it was, at last, the opening morning of bow season. Mr. Forrest had picked me up early that Saturday morning so that we could still-hunt one of his favorite "honey holes."

As I had learned over the past few weeks, still hunting was not at all what it sounded like. Instead of sitting still, you walked around slowly and quietly, looking for deer. So, the name didn't make a lot of sense to me. Seems to me that still hunting would be a better name for what you do in a tree stand than for being up and walking around. But, when I asked Mr. Forrest about it, he smiled and said, "You sure do think a lot, don't you?" before trying to give me an answer. "To be honest with you, son, I don't know why it's called still hunting. It just is. Maybe it's because you're moving so slowly and quietly that it ain't that much different from being still. Or maybe it's because you stop and remain still every few steps, slowly looking around for anything that might be a deer. But no matter what it's called, that's what we're going to do. We are going to get out there and just disappear into the trees," Mr. Forrest had explained to me a few weeks back. And that was the last I asked or wondered about it.

Still hunting is what we'd be doing today—on this first hunt of the season. Again, I wasn't the one with the bow and wouldn't be the one doing the shooting. I was the "student," Mr. Forrest had said as we drove to our hunting spot that morning. "And," he had added, "you'll learn a lot if you pay attention. Rule number one is to move slowly. Rule number two is to move quietly. Remember," he continued, "the best camouflage is being still because, more than anything else, deer see movement. And they can see it even when you think they aren't looking, Parker. My eyes and your eyes are set on the front of our heads and are always looking at the same thing at the same time— pretty much whatever is just right in front of us," he explained while pointing at the car that was in front of us. "But a deer's eyes are on the sides of their heads," he continued, moving his hand off to the side of his face, eventually pointing to the bed of his truck, while saying, "which means they can almost see clear back behind themselves. And they can pick up movement even when you think there is no way in the world they could see you—that they must be looking away."

So, as we began our slow creep through the woods that morning—just as the sun was starting to turn the sky from black to dark blue—I tried my best to remember all of these things. It was easy enough to move slowly because I could only move at the speed Mr. Forrest was moving—since he was just a few steps in front of me. But, moving quietly was more of a struggle. With almost every step, I was cracking a branch or crunching a leaf. I was expecting Mr. Forrest to turn around any minute and tell me to be more careful, but he never did. Maybe he knew that he didn't need to. It was pretty obvious I was making too much noise.

While I knew we'd be walking slowly, I was surprised at just how slowly we were moving. We'd take maybe three steps—sometimes two—and stop. Mr. Forrest had told me that deer know the difference between a human walking and another animal walking. "They know when it's a two-legged critter," he said. "We just sound different. But, when you only take two or three steps at a time, it's harder for them to pick up on that." And now that we were walking this way, I could kind of see what he meant.

He had also told me something else crazy—so crazy that I wasn't sure I really believed it. He said, "While normally we want to move as slowly as we can, taking two or three steps at a time, stopping to look and listen, and stopping so that the deer can't figure out we're one of those smelly critters with two legs, there are times when, for whatever reason, you can't walk slowly. Maybe you are trying to hustle to get to a certain spot you really want to hunt, or maybe you see a deer off in the distance and need to close the gap before it moves away. So, what do you do then?" he had asked without giving me a chance to answer.

"Well, I never had a good answer for that either," he admitted, "until I ran across this book by a man named Asbell—Fred Asbell. Because in that book, he talked about something he called 'deer walking.' And while it seemed sort of silly to me at first, the more I thought about it, and the more I tried it, the more I realized it actually worked."

"You see, Parker, when you and I walk through the woods, we make a certain sound—especially when we are walking in leaves. And it sounds like, 'Crunch, crunch, crunch, crunch, crunch'—just one step after another, all in rhythm, without any pauses. 'Crunch, crunch, crunch, crunch, crunch,'" he repeated. "But a deer sounds different when it walks—because it has four legs, not two. It sounds more like, 'crunch, crunch… crunch, crunch… crunch, crunch…'—so two steps and a pause, two more steps and a pause. Well, this Asbell feller figured out that he could imitate the whole crunch-crunch-pause sound by getting each of his steps to sound like two steps. To do that, he said you bring your foot to the ground with your toes pointing downward and hitting first—that's the first crunch," Mr. Forrest had explained as he lifted his foot high off the ground and brought it down toes first, still keeping the heel up. "And then," he continued, "as soon as your toes have touched the ground and made that crunch sound in the leaves, pop your heel down onto the ground quickly afterward and make a second crunch sound with it. That's how it works," he said with a smile before demonstrating it to me for several steps.

Well, that might have been how it worked, but after hearing him describe it and watching him do it, I was pretty doubt-ful that it could *actually* work. Not really. Not in the woods on a real deer. No way. To be honest, I was sort of wondering if he was just messin' with me like old men tend to do from time to time.

Little did I know, I'd soon find out he was telling the truth.

# Chapter 30

After taking two or three steps at a time for close to two hours, Mr. Forrest came to a sudden stop and moved himself with another half-step to the side, right up against a tree. Using his head, he motioned for me to step to the side as well, so I tucked in behind him and waited. I didn't know for sure what was going on, but I knew something had gotten his attention, and I was hoping it was a deer.

That's when he turned his head back toward me, keeping it hidden behind the tree, and whispered, "Parker, there are three does down in this bottom over here. They are feeding under that big acorn tree. Our wind is perfect, and if I can take five more steps without being heard or seen, I'll have some cover that will help me slip up on them. They're not fifty yards away. I want you to stay here and watch. Don't move a muscle, and don't make a sound. Okay?"

I was too scared to answer because that would have been making a sound. So, I just nodded and gave him a thumbs up before watching him turn away and take the quietest step I could ever imagine with all these leaves on the ground. Even though he told me not to move a muscle, I inched slowly to the tree and peered around it to watch as he took at least two minutes to make the five steps he needed to duck behind the cover of some brush.

Once there, Mr. Forrest looked back at me—almost like he wanted to be sure I was watching. And then he used his head to motion down toward his feet like he was trying to tell me something. I wasn't sure what it was until I watched him take that first step. He was doing the deer walk! "Crunch, crunch... crunch, crunch... crunch, crunch..." I heard him as he moved down toward the deer.

But then, after a few minutes, when he had cut his distance to the deer in half—down to about 25 yards—I couldn't hear him anymore. The wind and the sounds the woods were making because of the wind were completely drowning out the sound of his footsteps. He had mentioned that on the drive in today, and he was right! And I knew that was why the deer hadn't heard us.

But now he was close, and when I saw all their heads pop up from feeding to turn and look in his direction, I just knew he was busted. Which is why I was surprised that he just kept walking, moving slowly, pausing every couple of steps, and most certainly catching a glimpse when he could of the does who seemed more curious about his footfalls than nervous. In fact, eventually, I saw them, one by one, wag their tails just a bit, calmly put their heads back down, and resume their feeding. And this was when he was only fifteen yards away!

I couldn't believe it. He had been telling the truth! And he was about to shoot one of these does!

# Chapter 31

Mr. Forrest was coming to the end of the line of cover he had been using—he had about two more of his "deer steps" left. And I knew that when the cover was gone, it would be time for him to shoot. So, I watched as he made those two last steps. It seemed like forever, and my heart was pumping like I was the one about to shoot.

But then, in one smooth motion, Mr. Forrest took one final step, raised his bow as he did, and drew back as he raised it. One of the does was standing perfectly broadside to him, and I watched her leap at either the sound of the bow or the striking of the arrow. She took off like she had been shot out of a rifle, and after only about two seconds—when she made it out of my sight—I glanced back toward Mr. Forrest, who was already looking up at me with a big smile on his face.

———

"Dad, you just wouldn't have believed it!" I insisted over and over again after Mr. Forrest dropped me off at Sticks and Strings so that he could go home and process the doe. "He was like a ninja, Dad! He was like a deer-hunting ninja!"

That made my dad laugh and got my mom laughing, too. "A deer-hunting ninja," she chuckled. "That must've been something to see."

"It was!" I continued, still excited. "I just couldn't believe it. He was probably only twelve yards away when he took the shot. And they never knew he was there!"

"Son," my dad began with a happy smile, "I told you he was the real deal. I'm kind of jealous I wasn't there to see it. But I'm not surprised at all. And I'm also not surprised he downplayed the whole thing when he dropped you off, insisting that the deer were dumb and that he just got lucky."

"No, Dad, he's not lucky. He's good. Crazy good!" I insisted.

"Well, I'm glad you're getting the chance to learn from him," Dad continued. "And I'm also glad that after thinking the world was going to come to an end since you weren't going to be the one doing the shooting this year, you are so excited now. I figured you would be if you got to see something like that. Hunting from the ground raises the excitement a bit, doesn't it?"

"Uh, yeah," I replied with a silly look on my face. "My heart was pounding just watching it all from fifty yards away!"

"Well, I'm glad you had a good time today. And I'm glad you see how much Mr. Forrest has to teach you. But I'm also glad he said the next hunting lesson would be for me—tomorrow after church," Dad said with a smile that was mostly meant to rub it in my face.

But it didn't bother me. I wanted him to see the ninja at work with his very own eyes.

# Chapter 32

That next afternoon after church, Mr. Forrest stopped by to pick up my dad. He came in for a bit and helped me retell the story about yesterday's hunt. I still couldn't believe it, nor could I wait to get to school tomorrow to tell the Hunt Club Kids all about it. I also couldn't wait to hear the story Dad would have after his hunt with Mr. Forrest later this afternoon.

"Well, I guess we better get going," Mr. Forrest said after finishing up his story at the same time he finished the glass of sweet tea my mom had made him. "I've got a good idea of where we're going, but we'll need to see what the wind is doing in there before we decide exactly where we're sitting," he said as he stood up.

"Well, be careful and have a good time," my mom stood up and said.

"Yeah, and y'all get another one! That'd be two in two days!" I added.

"Y'all? You ain't coming?" Mr. Forrest asked me while glancing at my dad. "When I said this next lesson was for you," he continued, now talking just to Dad, "I didn't mean that the boy couldn't come. I just meant that I had some things I wanted to show you—stuff that the two of you could use together next time you take him out."

"Well..." my dad began before I interrupted him.

"I'll be right back," I shouted as I ran toward the stairs. "Let me change clothes. I'll be right back!"

"Okay, we'll be in the truck," Dad laughed as I ran up the stairs.

So, I quickly grabbed the same clothes I wore yesterday. Mr. Forrest had told me to wear a plaid shirt and some pants that would blend into the woods. "Again, I ain't saying that camo doesn't work," he had said. "But I want you to learn that moving slowly and quietly is what's most important. So, no camo for now. Okay? Not until you see for yourself."

I had agreed, and it certainly had worked yesterday. And as I ran down the stairs and hopped in the truck, I was hoping it would work today as well.

———————

We were in a different spot this afternoon. And that wasn't the only thing that was going to be different. Today, we'd be sitting still, using some natural cover like a ground blind. Plus, unlike yesterday, Mr. Forrest wouldn't be doing the shooting. My dad would.

Dad had been practicing a lot with his bow, too. And he was shooting good—really good—all the way out to thirty yards!

But, as Mr. Forrest reminded us, his rule was twenty yards or closer. And my dad made sure I knew that he was only shooting from thirty for fun and just in case he ever wanted to shoot in some 3D tournaments. But he assured us both that he would never, ever shoot at a deer from that far. "Not with a bow like this," he insisted.

"You know what's been funny to me over the years?" Mr. Forrest added. "It's funny how different we traditional archers are from other fellas. Guys who hunt with rifles and compound bows like to brag about how far away the deer was when they shot it. I hear they are shooting them out past sixty yards with a compound. And I've got friends who have taken deer out past three hundred yards with a rifle. But we guys who shoot traditional bows like to brag, too. Only we don't brag about how far away the deer was when we shot. We brag about how close they were when we shot. That's what it's about for us. And just like we find it hard to believe that someone shot a deer at three hundred yards, that same guy finds it hard to believe that we shot one at eight yards. We think they're lyin', and they think we are. But the truth is getting them in close, the way we have to do it—and the way we like to do it—is just a completely different way of thinking from most of the fellas out there in the deer woods. And just like taking a long shot is tough, taking a short one is tough, too—probably tougher."

———————

With three hours of daylight left, Mr. Forrest, my dad, and I were set up in a dried-up creek bottom that was surrounded by ten white oak trees that were raining acorns. One bonked me on the head at one point during the hunt, and it was all I could do not to scream. We were all dressed in our plaid shirts and woods-colored pants. And Mr. Forrest had set up Dad in front of a tree and helped "brush him in" using some limbs that were already lying on the ground. They had also used some black string to pull a couple of smaller trees over out to the side of my dad's setup. When they were finished and my dad slipped into place, I was amazed at how well he was hidden.

Mr. Forrest and I moved back fifteen yards or so from my dad and propped our chairs up against a tree that was already well-covered on all sides by thick brush. You could easily see where the deer had been tearing up the acorns in that creek bottom. The ground was all torn up. And so, my hopes were really high that Dad and I would go home with a deer of our own that day.

# Chapter 33

But one hour passed—and nothing. Then another hour passed—and still nothing. And when that last full hour of daylight was almost gone, I was almost ready to give up hope. That's when Mr. Forrest nudged me and nodded at the hillside out in front of my dad.

We were in the woods, and it was getting dark. So, seeing out too far in front of us was getting tough. But I was able to make out two does working their way down the hillside. One was about twenty yards in front of the other. And even closer to my dad than that by the time I saw her.

Just like yesterday, my heart started racing. We probably had twenty minutes of shooting light left. And this doe was moving slowly, but steadily, down the hill toward my dad—right into the shooting lane we had hoped one would pass through.

When getting set up, Mr. Forrest took a minute to teach us some good stuff about shooting lanes and about getting set up to shoot through them. He had to whisper and couldn't talk long, but what he said made complete sense.

He said, "We want to make sure that your shooting lane is set up so that the deer is already looking away and quartering away when it passes by. You also can't position your chair so that you're facing directly at the spot where you'll want to take the shot. You need your bow shoulder pointed that way. So, turn your chair so that the shooting lane is off to your left. Because that's how you'll draw and shoot your bow."

"And," he added, before the two of us stepped back to leave my dad alone, "you also need to draw your bow a few times once we get out of here—to make sure nothing is in your way. And you might want to do it every now and then during the hunt—to keep your arms from getting stiff. You don't want to figure that out when you've got a deer standing in front of you."

The doe in front walked straight into where my dad was hoping a deer would pass that day. But he was also set up the way he was with the hope that one would pass through from left to right or from right to left—not straight toward him. As it was, and as it remained for at least five minutes, he had no shot—even though the doe was now inside ten yards. Mr. Forrest and I were watching the whole thing play out, and I cannot imagine how fast my dad's heart was beating because mine was going one hundred miles per hour.

I knew he didn't have a shot, but I also knew there were only about ten minutes of daylight left. Not to mention, things couldn't last as they were for much longer— the doe was just too close. And remember, there was another one working in behind her. Things were about to blow up.

And they did. Not because the doe smelled my dad like I thought she would, but because my dad "tried to make something happen," he explained later, "even when I knew I shouldn't. I had made up my mind that the next time she put her head back down to eat, I was going to start raising my bow. But I didn't move it two inches before she was on me."

Mr. Forrest and I saw all of this playing out from our hiding spot. We saw Dad lift the bow, we saw the doe raise her head, and we saw her eyes lock onto him. We watched as they had a staring competition for about a minute. And, of course, we watched as she and her friend ran back the way they had come.

While it was pretty frustrating to me, Dad wasn't frustrated at all. "That was the most exciting hunt I've ever done in my life!" he announced when we made our way back to the truck. "I mean it," he continued. "I've never had a deer that close to me while I was on the ground. That was insane. And she had no idea I was there—not until I blew it, at least."

"Well, you ain't the first one to get worked up like that and do something you knew better than doing. I've done it before myself," Mr. Forrest admitted. "I do it every year. But I do hope that both of you see what hunting on the ground can do to you—how it changes things. I doubt very seriously either of you would have gotten near that worked-up over a doe had you been sitting in a shooting house, looking out over a greenfield, at a doe standing a hundred or more yards away. You just wouldn't have. There's something special, boys, about being on the ground with a traditional bow, huntin' them up close and personal like we did today. Something special, indeed."

He was right. And I was sure ready to experience it for myself—with the bow in my hand. But I still had nearly a year to wait.

# Chapter 34

I didn't have to wait long for our next hunt, though. Every few days, either me and Mr. Forrest, or the two of us plus my dad, were out hunting together. Dad quickly redeemed himself from the mistake he had made on that doe he had inside ten yards. Just a few days later, in a different location, almost the exact same scenario was playing out. Once again, Mr. Forrest and I were watching from a distance. This time, Dad kept his cool and didn't try to rush the shot. His patience paid off when the doe directly in front of him turned around to make sure the doe behind her was still there. That gave him a beautiful quartering-away shot, which he put right where it needed to be.

Then, just a couple of days later, on a still hunt by himself, Dad spotted a small buck a hundred yards off—walking down a trail he had found while scouting a few weeks earlier. Fortunately, the wind was whipping pretty good, which meant that Dad was able to hustle to an ambush spot without alerting the deer. Once set up, he waited just a few minutes before he was able to surprise the buck when it walked over the top of a little knoll—totally oblivious to his presence.

Needless to say, Dad and I were learning a lot—a whole lot—about what it meant to hunt with a traditional bow and in traditional ways. Which was good because the group hunt with the other Hunt Club Kids at Wyatt's house was fast approaching, and I wanted us to be ready.

"I can't wait," Jet said one day at lunch.

"Me neither," Mason agreed. "I'm going to find that monster buck's brother. Y'all just watch and see."

"We're all looking forward to it," Wyatt promised. "We've been talking about it for months, and my dad has some good spots picked out for all of you and your dads."

"He knows we'll be hunting with my dad's traditional bow, right?" I asked, scared they had forgotten.

"Yeah," Wyatt answered. "He thinks that's so cool. In fact, he's planning to talk to your dad about getting a bow built for himself."

"Well, my dad would love that," I answered. "He keeps saying that we're not selling as many as he thought we would."

"But all the deer y'all have killed this year have been with your dad's bow, right? That's all y'all are hunting with now?" Mason asked.

"Yep. That's all we're doing now," I answered. "Just our traditional bows. Which is why I can't hunt this year. Dad won't let me hunt with mine until I'm twelve. But he's already killed two this year, and it's been fun to be there with him. And hopefully, we'll get another one on Saturday—maybe even shoot that big one right out from under Mason's nose," I said as I elbowed him in the arm.

———————

Well, as it turned out, Dad and I didn't get the brother of the record book buck Wyatt and his dad had killed last season. But we did kill the only deer that day—and he was nothing to be ashamed of. Yes, while all the other boys were hunting with rifles, Dad and I still-hunted through one section of Wyatt's property and snuck up on a nice eight-point that was bedded down on the side of a ridge. He never knew we were there, and he may have never even stood up for my dad to take a shot if Dad hadn't bleated at him.

When he did stand, the shot was perfect, from about eighteen yards. The buck ran downhill about fifty yards and fell easily within our sight.

The Hunt Club Kids and their dads couldn't believe it. And before we left, they all said they wanted bows. And all the boys said they wanted Mr. Forrest to teach them how to shoot.

―――――――

Thanks to the orders from the Hunt Club Kids and their dads, Sticks and Strings was busier building bows than it ever had been. But as much as those orders helped, things still weren't where they needed to be with the business. And in a family meeting, Dad told us he was starting to get worried.

"We're not there yet," he explained, "but if we can't figure out a way to start selling more bows, we're not going to be able to keep things going much longer. And I may have to seriously consider taking up my old boss on his offer about that flying job in Texas."

# Chapter 35

Over the next few days, it became more and more clear to me that the threat of having to move to Texas had really returned. I over-heard my parents talking—mostly whisper-ing—about troubles with the business. It was the middle of November now, and I had heard my dad saying that our holiday sales would make or break things. "Either we have a good November and December," I heard him saying to my mom, "or else I'll have to make the call." I knew what he meant by "the call." He was talking about calling his old boss to get his old job back, which meant moving to Texas.

And so, I was worried—very worried. But I didn't say anything to anyone because I really just didn't want to talk about it. I did pray, though, which my Sunday School teacher says is how we talk to God. So, I guess I did talk to someone. I asked him to please do something again—like he had done last time when my dad met Mr. Forrest at the airport and ended up starting Sticks and Strings. We were all so happy about it. None of us wanted to move, and God had made a way for us to stay. We all believed that! And now, for a reason I couldn't understand, it was starting to look like we were going to have to move again. But I didn't want to think about it, and I didn't want to talk about it, so I didn't—except with God. Other than that, I just pretended like it wasn't happening.

It was always in the back of my mind, though. And I was having a hard time enjoying anything—even hunting! While Dad and I hunted together and with Mr. Forrest several more times in November and December, and even though both Dad and Mr. Forrest had killed more deer, I didn't enjoy those hunts as much as I had before. There was too much to think about—too much to worry about.

In the back of my Bible, there was a section that pointed you to certain verses when you were having certain kinds of problems. I had never really noticed it before. But one day, in the middle of all this, I did. And I saw there was a section about feeling worried and what verses could help with that. It listed Philippians 4:6-7, which says: "Do not be anxious about anything, but in everything by prayer and supplication with thanksgiving let your requests be made known to God. And the peace of God, which surpasses all understanding, will guard your hearts and your minds in Christ Jesus."

I knew that being anxious meant the same thing as worrying. And so, I knew this verse was talking to me—that God was talking to me. And so, I answered back, saying, "God, I don't want to worry. But I can't help it. I don't want to move. Just like before, I am scared about the thought of that—about leaving my friends, about leaving my school, about leaving my church, and about leaving my house. But this verse says if I tell you about these worries, you will give me peace—which I need. So, I am telling you that I am worried and praying that you'll help me not be—no matter what happens."

I didn't feel better right away. But as the days passed in November and December, even as I continued to hear my parents talk about how bad the business was doing, I worried about it less and less and knew that no matter what happened, everything would be alright.

# Chapter 36

All the other Hunt Club Kids had gotten Sticks and Strings bows for Christmas. And by the middle of January, we were all regularly practicing together with Mr. Forrest. But the threat of having to move to Texas was very real at this point. I had pretty much accepted that it was going to happen. I think Piper and my parents had, too. I was okay with it now, though. And it seemed like they were as well. None of us wanted to move, and we had all done our best so that we wouldn't have to move, but things with the business just didn't go as well as we had hoped.

"Selling traditional bows today is probably a little like what it must have been like trying to sell horses and wagons after the car was invented," I heard my dad tell my mom one afternoon with a sad laugh.

"Well, we gave it our best shot," she answered. "That's all we could do. We tried."

"Yeah, we tried," he agreed. "I just wish it would have worked. I hate having to do this to the kids. I just hate it. And Parker is going to take it the worst."

Of course, that made me feel bad. They had enough to worry about without worrying about me. I was going to be fine. I had already decided that. So, when I got a chance later that day, I let Dad know it without letting him know I had overheard their conversation.

"Hey, Dad," I said. "I've heard they have some really good baseball in Texas. Do you think I'll be good enough to make a team?"

"Are you kidding?" he asked. "Those boys won't know what's happened to them when you step on the mound," he continued. "And then when you get up to the plate, they'll be calling in scouts from the Rangers and the Astros," he laughed.

"I'm good with moving, Dad," was my answer. "It's going to be okay. We don't need to worry about it. It's all going to be fine."

"Well, Parker," he replied, "I appreciate you saying that because I have been worried. And a lot of my worry has been about you and how you'd handle it."

"I'll be fine, Dad. Really, I'll be fine," I assured him. "We'll still be able to hunt. And I'll still be able to play baseball. And I'll still get to see the Hunt Club Kids when we come back for the holidays. It'll all be fine."

"I agree," he answered. "But I'm still trying to keep us here. It's going to take a miracle at this point. But miracles do happen, and so I've been praying that one would," he said right as Mason, Jet, and Wyatt came barreling through the door, ending our conversation.

It was time for our practice session with Mr. Forrest, and Jet's mom had picked up the other boys and dropped them off. Mr. Forrest was already back on the range, and so after messing around for a couple of minutes, we all headed back that way to get started.

They were all still shooting at the line of white tape, the same way I had done at first. And even though I had advanced beyond that, Mr. Forrest had me shooting at it again, too—to keep things easy. "Ain't gonna hurt you, son," he insisted.

The other boys had been practicing with me now for a few weeks, and we were all shooting good—really good.

I had no way of knowing how important this was about to be.

# Chapter 37

When our practice session wrapped up that day, we were all happy with how well we were doing. I was really impressed with how fast the other boys were catching on. Mr. Forrest was happy, too. "Looks like I am going to make bowhunters out of you boys after all," he joked.

"Thank you for your help," Mason answered.

"Yeah, we really appreciate it," Wyatt agreed.

Then, after walking over to his workbench and gathering up his lunchbox and a few other things, Mr. Forrest said, "Well, let's call it a night. You boys are doing good. I'll see you in a couple of days. And, if you keep shooting like you're shooting, it won't be long before we turn that target around," he said with a smile as he headed toward the door. "And y'all try to stay warm. It's cold out here!" he added before the door closed behind him.

The building we had chosen for Sticks and Strings was old—really old. And, before it became clear that the business probably wasn't going to make it, my parents were planning a lot of upgrades. One of the things it certainly needed was a new heater. That had become clear to us as soon as winter arrived. But there was no need to worry about it now. We wouldn't be here for the next winter.

Nevertheless, the cold drove me and the rest of the boys to the office part of the building—where my mom and dad handled all the business stuff. My dad was supposed to be back there and was going to take us all home. But when we made it to his office, he wasn't there. And while the other boys looked at some of the hunting magazines lying on his desk, I called him to see where he was.

"Parker, I'm so sorry. I had an errand to run and got stuck in traffic. I'm just a few minutes away. I tried to catch Mr. Forrest before he left, but you know he never has his phone turned on. Anyway, y'all just sit tight in my office, and I'll be there as quickly as I can."

While I was on the phone, Wyatt had gone back out of the office to get his bow. He had left it out by the shooting range. But almost as soon as I put the phone down, he came bursting back into the office, screaming "There's smoke! And a fire! Hurry! Let's get out of here!"

So, we all grabbed our bows and ran out of the office and into the part of the building where the bows were built. And I couldn't believe it when I saw it. Wyatt was telling the truth. There was a fire, and it was getting bigger by the second. But somehow, I knew what to do.

Several months ago, right after we moved to the building, Mom and Piper had insisted on some bathroom upgrades. While I wouldn't admit it to them, the old bathrooms were pretty bad—even for a boy. But while the work was being done, I learned that the white pipes running across the ceilings of our building were the water pipes. I also heard the plumber and my dad talking about needing to install a sprinkler system in the building as soon as possible. But that hadn't happened yet. We just couldn't afford it.

But boy, did we need a sprinkler system right now. The fire was spreading fast, and I knew if it got to the stack of staves that were neatly organized not too far away from where the fire had started—which happened to be at the old heater—that would be it. This building and my family's business would be gone.

Thankfully, in that very moment, almost out of nowhere, an idea came into my brain about how we could make a sprinkler system—and make one fast.

"Wait!" I yelled to the other boys, who were running toward the door just as they should have been. "Listen to me! And listen carefully!" I continued to scream.

"No, Parker! We've got to go," they screamed.

But I didn't stop my instructions.

"Do you see those white pipes running across the ceiling? Take your bows and shoot arrows into it! Just pretend it's the white line on the target Mr. Forrest has had you aiming at! Shoot as many holes in those pipes as you can!"

Before I finished, I was already drawing my bow with an arrow nocked and ready to fly. And, within half a second of reaching the corner of my mouth with my middle finger, the arrow was on its way. When it hit the pipe, there was an explosion of water. But I was too busy nocking another arrow and drawing back to give it much attention.

That's when I heard Jet say, "Do what he says!"

And before I knew it, arrows were flying from each of their bows, and water was coming down everywhere. Once all our arrows were gone, I screamed, "Let's go!" And we made it outside right as my dad was pulling in.

"What in the world is going on?" he asked frantically as we were running toward him. He could see we were soaking wet and all very upset.

"Dad! The building is on fire!" I yelled. "It's all going to burn up! Call the fire trucks!"

He immediately pulled his phone from his pocket and called 911.

"Are you okay? Are you all okay?" he asked as he checked each of us over and put us in his truck to warm us up. We were all soaking wet, and it was freezing cold.

# Chapter 38

By the time the firemen arrived, the fire was already out. Our sprinkler system had done the job.

Mr. Forrest had heard what was going on and had made his way back. He was as upset as we were. First, he felt bad that he had left us, but he thought my dad was in his office, too—just like we did. But he also felt bad because he knew this would be the end—the end of Sticks and Strings. There's no doubt that Mr. Forrest wanted this business to work as much as we did. He had spent his entire life building, shooting, and hunting with traditional bows, and it was hard for him to watch it all go up in smoke—literally.

But eventually, after turning off the water to the building, the firemen let us go back inside to check out the damage. There was water everywhere. The whole building was flooded. Things were floating all around us, and it was a sad sight to see. But it wasn't nearly as bad as it could have been. Not only could this mess be cleaned up and everything put back together, but this building, which was old and very important to our town, was still standing. That meant a lot to Mr. Forrest, too.

Eventually, my mom arrived, along with the parents of the other Hunt Club Kids. Everyone was hugging, and so happy nothing worse had happened. It certainly could have. And so, they spent a lot of time lecturing us about how dumb it was for us not to just run. And they were right. The truth is we should have run. We should have dropped everything and run because the only things in that building that couldn't have been replaced were the four boys—me, Wyatt, Jet, and Mason. We all knew that's what we were supposed to do. And it was beyond dumb to stay and do what we did. It wasn't worth the risk. Everyone explained that to us over and over again, and we all promised that we would never do anything like that again—not for any reason.

But eventually, it was time to go. "We've got a big mess to clean up tomorrow," my dad said as he looked around the place one last time. "And so, we're going to need to try and get some sleep."

After each of the other boy's dads promised to help with the cleanup tomorrow, we all headed toward the door, where we witnessed another part of the miracle.

Because at the door, we were bombarded by news reporters with their cameras. They wanted to know the whole story—every detail. And as we told it, more and more arrived, from other towns even. They were amazed at what we had done— me and the other Hunt Club Kids.

And so, in spite of our stupidity, the story about what we did that night went viral. People from all over the world heard about it. Pictures of me and the other Hunt Club Kids holding our bows and videos of us explaining what we had done were being seen and shared all over the world.

———

And that's when the orders started rolling in—and I mean rolling in. The website crashed a couple of times over the next few weeks. The phones were ringing off the hook. And my parents had to hire dozens of people to manage it all.

Sticks and Strings had been saved. And, once again, we weren't moving to Texas.

# Chapter 39

While there were still a few weeks of hunting season left after the fire, it was honestly the last thing on any of our minds. We were busy not only putting the business and the building back together, but with all the new orders and with all the new people, things were just too crazy to even think about hunting. It was crazy in a good way.

When things started to settle down a few months later, and Mom and Dad had the business running smoothly—and doing very well—I was sitting with my dad in his office one day after school when Mr. Forrest knocked and walked in.

"Well, boys," he began, "this has been about the most amazing thing I have ever seen. I'm just glad that I've gotten to be a small part of it."

"You haven't been a small part of it, Forrest," my dad interrupted. "You've probably been the most important part of it. Without you, none of this would have been possible."

"Well, I don't know about all that," Mr. Forrest continued. "But from the very beginning, I told you that when the time was right, I'd step away and leave it to you. Well, from the looks of things out there," he said as he pointed out to all the people building and shipping bows, "I'd say the time is right. Yes, siree, I'd say the time is right."

"But," he continued while holding up his hand to stop Dad or me from interrupting him, "that don't mean I won't be around. And that certainly don't mean we can't hunt together anymore. In fact," he said as he turned and looked at me and pointed at the bow in my hands, "me and this boy here still have one job to complete before my work here is officially done. We're gonna get him a deer with that there bow we built. And if I remember correctly, your dad says you'll be old enough this fall, right?"

I nodded and smiled, looking over at my dad to make sure he was nodding too. Thankfully, he was.

Then, after spending some time telling Mr. Forrest how much we both appreciated him, we began to make plans for hunting together that fall.

# Chapter 40

Over the next several months, me and the rest of the Hunt Club Kids got together a few days a week to shoot our bows with Mr. Forrest. That was still part of what he said he needed to do before he was officially done here. "I've got to finish teaching these young'uns to shoot."

One day, as Mr. Forrest and I were watching the rest of them shoot, he caught me looking as he watched and smiled at how good the other boys were doing.

"Parker, I've been wanting to say this for a while," he leaned over and said after he caught me looking. "But now seems like the right time. So here it is," he continued. "Even though what you did that night when you put out the fire was dumb, and even though I still want to kick you in the tail for it—and I mean kick you hard—by doing what you did, Parker, you not only saved this old building and your family's business along with it, but you may have also saved this old way of hunting that I love. And for that, son, I am forever grateful—to you."

I didn't really know what to say. So, I just gave him a half smile and a nod. He knew what it meant and patted me on the head to show me that he knew.

———————

Before I knew it, fifth grade was done, and sixth grade was beginning. And not long after school started, I turned twelve—in September—which meant that I could hunt this season. That was what my dad had said. And Mr. Forrest and I were going to hold him to it.

But we didn't have to hold him to anything. He knew what he promised and was as excited about it as I was. In fact, it was the first thing he mentioned to me when he woke me up on the morning of my birthday.

"You ready to hunt with that bow?" he asked as he nudged me for the tenth time, trying to wake me up.

Those were definitely the right words because I hopped up and said, "You know it!" as soon as they came out of his mouth.

"Happy Birthday, son," he smiled when my feet hit the floor. "I can't believe you're twelve. And I'm serious about the hunting. I'm excited about it, too. And I know Mr. Forrest is as well. I really think you'll make it happen this year. You've been right there with both of us, and I know you're ready."

Of course, the season was still just over a month away. And so, I still had a little waiting to do. But I also had a lot of work to do.

If I was going to be the one doing the shooting this year, I was going to make sure I was ready. And so, that afternoon, I got real serious about practicing.

———

When things started to pick up at Sticks and Strings, my parents made a lot of improvements to the shop. We began, of course, with a new heater and a REAL sprinkler system. But we also did a lot of work to improve the shooting range. And so, not only did we have regular bullseye-style targets, but now we also had a few deer targets set up at different yardages. And that's what I began to shoot at.

Mr. Forrest had always emphasized the importance of "picking a spot" and "staring a hole through it," but it was much easier to pick a spot on a bullseye-type target with a little round circle in the center than it was on a target shaped like a deer. He explained that to me one day when he came in and saw how frustrated I was with it.

"I can't hit anything," I complained when he walked up. "I don't even know what I am thinking if I really believe I'm ready to shoot a deer with this stupid thing," I continued while I shook my bow out in front of him.

"You know," Mr. Forrest began, "I remember teaching a boy to shoot not too long ago that got all upset like this and was ready to give up. What was the boy's name again? I think it started with a 'P,'" he said as he moved his head to look into my eyes that were doing the best they could not to look at him.

Of course, I knew he was talking about me. And I knew he was right.

"Listen," he continued, "I'm just messing with you. I know hitting these deer targets can be a little tougher. But I also know that you'll get it. Just stick with it."

So, I did. And over the next few days, I was hitting them right where I was looking. And by the time deer season opened in the middle of October, I was confident about what would happen if one came into range.

# Chapter 41

"Parker, Mr. Forrest is going to be here in thirty minutes," my mom whispered as she woke me up on that first morning of bow season. "I've got breakfast ready for you, but you need to hurry up and get going."

I didn't need any more nudging. I had been waiting on this day for over a year. And so, I was out of bed and in my hunting clothes in what must have looked like one smooth motion.

---

My dad was joining us that morning, but he would be hunting alone while Mr. Forrest would be with me, finishing what he started, as he explained it. Once again, just like with the business, I think Mr. Forrest wanted this hunt to work out as much as I did. He really wanted me to get a deer with my bow, and he was doing—just as he had been doing—everything he could to make sure that happened.

"I've got a good feeling about today, Parker. I really do. Yes, sir, I really do," he said as we rode along with my dad driving. "But the goal is not only to get you a deer today," he continued. "We also want to show your dad up in the process," he said with a smile, glancing over to my dad to make sure he was listening. "Yes, sir, if you remember, I set him up with an easy hunt his first time out with us. I let him get all hidden in front of that big ol' tree with all that thick brush out in front of him. But that ain't how we're doin' it today—not for your first hunt. No, sir. Today, we're going to still-hunt 'em."

"Now wait a minute!" my dad protested with a smile, "that doe came within ten yards of me that day! There ain't nothing easy about that!"

"Mustn't have been too easy," Mr. Forrest laughed, "cause you sure 'nuff ran her off!"

"But I redeemed myself like two days later!" my dad fought back, still laughing.

"Yeah, but that setup was even easier," Mr. Forrest joked. "We could have hidden an elephant in that spot, and the deer wouldn't have known it!"

That made us all laugh, but I knew that today was going to be tough. And I wondered why Mr. Forrest was making it tougher. I really thought we'd probably just go back to one of those spots he had just mentioned. The ones we had taken my dad to last year. But, for whatever reason, he was making it hard. I thought about asking him why, but I decided to trust that he knew what he was doing—which I would soon find out he did.

———————

After parking the truck and gathering our gear, Dad wished me luck and headed off in one direction while me and Mr. Forrest stayed put for a minute to have a talk.

"Alright, Parker. Here's what we're going to do," he began, just as the sun was starting to turn the sky from black to blue. "We are going to follow this old logging road," he continued while pointing to it, "until it leads us down to this creek bed I want us to hunt. The water doesn't really flow down there, but it's almost always damp, and the ground is perfect for still hunting. We can follow it for a long ways, a few hours at least, before it leads us to another road we can follow back to the truck for lunch—hopefully dragging a deer behind us. How does that sound?"

It sounded good to me. And I told him so. I still didn't really know what I was doing, so I was certainly following his lead—or at least I thought. Because when it was time to head out, and I tried to fall in behind him like I had always done, he whispered, "Not today. You're leading the way today. You've got the bow, and you're doing the shooting. Which means I'm following you. Now go on," he finished with a nod of his head that told me to start walking.

# Chapter 42

The walk on the logging road, down into the creek bed, took us about twenty minutes. It was still mostly dark on the way in, and the road made it easy to move quickly and quietly. But now that we were at the spot where we'd begin our actual hunting, I had to tell myself to slow down and quiet down.

I was happy that when I placed all my weight on my back foot, so that I could feel the ground with the toes of my front foot, I discovered that Mr. Forrest was right. We'd be able to move through here pretty quietly—the leaves were damp and soft. But I also knew that I didn't need to let that tempt me to move too quickly, as it was easy to do when you weren't making that much noise. Because the quickest way to get seen— whether you are a human or a deer—was by your movement. Which is why, whenever I think about still hunting, the goal, in my mind, is to move less than the deer are moving. Because if they are moving more than me, I have a better chance of seeing them first. Which was what still hunting was all about—seeing a deer before it sees you. And then, of course, not letting it see you at all.

So, I told myself to take two or three slow steps and stop. And I was constantly moving from one sort of cover to another. Of course, I knew that Mr. Forrest was right there, and if I needed to do anything differently, he would speak up.

But for the next hour, that is what I did— two or three steps from one tree to the next. I went slow enough that those steps would probably take ten seconds each. Then, after a few steps, I'd stop for at least a couple of minutes, sometimes ten, if the terrain around me looked like somewhere a deer might be moving.

There were ridges on both sides of us, and even though the woods were still green and lush this time of year, we had a pretty good view up both of the ridges running alongside the creek bed. So good, in fact, that I decided this is why Mr. Forrest had chosen this spot.

Well, at about an hour into it, while I had stopped against a tree to take a sip of water, I caught some movement out of the corner of my eye. Without thinking about it, I jerked my head in that direction, wishing I had moved more slowly as soon as I did it. Fortunately, my abrupt movement didn't scare off the three does who were walking about seventy-five yards out in front of us, just below the top of the ridgeline. They were coming our way, but we'd have to close the gap.

I looked back to Mr. Forrest, who was already looking at me to see what I was going to do—meaning that he had seen the deer, too. And when I nodded my head, showing him I was going to move their way, he responded with a nod of approval.

So, I crossed the dry creek bed as quietly as I could and began to pay more attention to where I was placing my each and every step through the much drier leaves. The wind was blowing some on this day, but not enough—I was afraid—to mask very much of the noise it'd be easy to make. Fortunately, the three deer were moving slowly, stopping to pick at leaves and acorns along the way. But I was beginning to worry that they weren't moving slowly enough and that I wouldn't be able to cut them off if I didn't hurry. The angle I had chosen just wasn't going to work out. And so, I picked up the pace—which also picked up the noise. I felt like I didn't have a choice, though. I had to make something happen.

Well, I made something happen, alright. I made the three does run off, huffing and puffing at me, alerting every other deer in the county that I was there. When I looked back at Mr. Forrest, he just smiled and shrugged before he gestured with his head for me to come back down toward him.

# Chapter 43

"Well, you got close," Mr. Forrest said with a grin. "That wasn't bad at all."

But I knew he was only trying to make me feel better. The truth is that it was bad. I sounded like a herd of buffalo moving up that hill. What was I even thinking? That was never going to work.

"This just isn't going to work!" I complained. "There's no way I'm going to kill a deer like this. It's a total waste of time."

He didn't answer at first. And I could tell he was thinking carefully about what he would say.

"Parker," Mr. Forrest began, "you can't give up every time you fail or every time something is hard. You won't get anywhere in life like that. What we're doing today is tough, just like learning to shoot your bow was tough. You almost quit that, too. Remember?"

I did. But I just kept staring off into the woods without acknowledging it.

"The truth is, you messed up just now," he continued—telling the truth. "But you're also out here doing something hard while most kids your age are at home, still asleep, after playing video games all night. And that says something about you. Something that doesn't surprise me at all, really, after knowing your family for a while now."

"Look at me, son," he said after a brief pause, also stepping around in front of me so that I could no longer avoid looking at him. "Tell me what your dad did when things got tough for him last year. Did he decide it was too hard—just too much—and give up? Or did he scratch and claw until the very last minute, doing whatever he could to find a way to keep from having to uproot your family from your home? What did he do, Parker?"

I knew the answer. And he knew I knew the answer. My dad hadn't given up. He never gave up.

"In fact, do you know what he was doing the night of the fire at the shop? Do you know where he was?" Mr. Forrest looked me straight in the eye and asked. "Yes, he got caught in traffic that night, but the whole truth is that he had been down at the bank trying one last time to convince them to loan him a bit more money so that he could keep things going—so that he could keep trying to make it work."

I didn't know what to say. So, I didn't say anything.

"That said," Mr. Forrest interrupted my thoughts, "if you want to give up, we can walk out of here right now. It won't take us long to get back to the truck. And when your dad comes out, we'll take you home. And I'll just hunt with him the rest of the afternoon. It's no big deal to me."

If he had told the truth when he said I had messed up, Mr. Forrest had not told the truth when he said it wasn't a big deal to him if I quit. I knew it was. He cared about me. And he was disappointed in me right now. He was disappointed that, once again, when I didn't do great at something—on my very first try—I was immediately ready to quit.

I knew I had a choice to make. And it was bigger than a choice about what I was going to do right now. It was a choice about how I would respond from this point forward when I failed at something. Would I give up? Or would I get up and try again?

Would I be a quitter? Or would I be like my dad?

Mr. Forrest just stood there and watched as I processed all this. The silence had lasted longer than was comfortable. Someone needed to say something. But I knew he had said everything he was going to say. So, it had to be me.

"You think we should press on down this creek bed?" I asked, saying it like nothing had ever happened. "Or do you have another spot you want to check out?"

He stared at me for a second or two before answering. "We've still got plenty to hunt down here," he said, also pretending that nothing had happened. "Why don't we press on, at least for another hour or so, and see what we run across?"

So, we did.

And less than forty-five minutes later, I caught some more movement—out of the other eye this time. It was a lone deer up on the other side of the creek bed. It was up on the ridge but not nearly as high as the three does had been before.

There was a tree just to my right, and I moved toward it with a single sideways step. From that position, I took a moment to catch my breath and think—something I didn't do last time. This deer, which also appeared to be a doe, was only about fifty yards away. But, unlike the does this morning, it wasn't really moving in any particular direction. It was just kind of browsing around in one spot, probably feeding on acorns.

After a minute or two of watching and observing, I had come up with a plan and was ready to make my move.

# Chapter 44

Just as I was about to take my first step, I realized Mr. Forrest had made his way up to me, without making a bit of noise. It was amazing how he could do that. He was close to silent in the woods.

"Parker," he whispered, "it's time for me to step away and let you take it from here—just like I did with your dad and with the business. You know what to do. I believe in you. Now, just go do it."

I wasn't sure I believed in myself as much as he did. But I gave him a nod, nocked an arrow, and took my first step away from the safety of the tree.

I knew from my many lessons in the woods with Mr. Forrest that even though it seems like the opposite of what would be true, the best way to approach a deer in the woods is straight on. They just see less of your movement that way. And so that's what I did.

While standing behind the tree down by the creek bed, I mapped out a path where I could walk from tree to tree straight toward the deer. I would move slowly and quietly. This time, I was willing, even, to take the chance that it might move away before I got there. Rushing things, the way I had done before, certainly hadn't worked. And so, this time, I decided I'd rather it just walk off than be spooked off like the does had been when I got in a hurry.

So, step after step, I moved as quietly and slowly as I could from tree to tree. I kept my eyes bouncing from the ground and back up to the deer. I was looking for any sign that it might be on to me. But it gave me none. It remained as comfortable as it had been back when I first saw it from down in the creek bed.

Forty yards away. Thirty-five yards away. Thirty yards away. Closer and closer, I crept. Everything was working according to plan—right until I made it to the tree that was about twenty-five yards away. Though I couldn't see the whole deer, it was obvious from its back half—which I could see from this position—that it had straightened and stiffened up for some reason. The wind was still good. So that wasn't it. Which meant it must have seen me or heard me.

My heart was racing now. I was close, but not close enough. I needed to get at least five yards closer, and preferably ten closer, if I wanted to be super comfortable with the shot. But the deer was tense now. And I didn't know what to do.

I wished Mr. Forrest was here with me to tell me. But he was twenty-five yards behind me, still standing and observing from behind the tree where I left him. I was on my own. I'd have to decide what to do. And that's when it hit me.

If the deer had seen me, it didn't know what I was. If it did, it would have run. And the same with if it heard me. If my footsteps had cracked a leaf or stick too loudly, that noise had not announced that it was made by a human. So, the best way I could relax this deer, I decided, was to make it think that whatever it heard or whatever it saw was just another deer. And I knew how to do that. I'd do the deer walk Mr. Forrest had taught me—at least to the next tree, which was only a few steps away.

Toe, then heel, I reminded myself. Toe, then heel. Two crunches, then a pause. Two more crunches, then another pause, I thought.

I took a deep breath and took my first deer step.

*Crunch, crunch* the leaves sounded out as my toes and heel came down upon them. I felt like my heart was going to stop beating, but I knew I couldn't stop there. I was too exposed. So, I took the next step, once again hearing the *crunch, crunch* sound out from under my foot. And then, after one more step, I had made it, and the deer hadn't bolted. Not yet, at least.

As I stood there and tried to calm myself down, I could now hear the deer moving, too. It surprised me how much it sounded like the footsteps I had just taken. And it must have thought the same! Because not only was it not running away from me, but it was, to my amazement, moving closer— like it wanted to see which of its friends had come for a visit.

I couldn't believe it!

# Chapter 45

One step, two steps, three steps. It was coming closer and closer. And so, I knew I had to get ready. Fortunately, I was not only behind a tree, but there was some waist-high brush just out in front of it, too. So, I positioned myself behind the tree, in a squatted position which completely concealed me behind the brush. And I didn't move a muscle. I was almost too scared to breathe.

I knew the deer was coming, so I peeked through the brush, anxiously waiting for it to appear. The rhythmic *crunch, crunch* of the leaves told me it was getting closer. And eventually, I saw its right front leg come down only about fifteen yards in front of me. It wasn't moving fast, but it also wasn't stopping between steps. And so, I knew I had to be ready to make my move—a move that would require me to rise from my squatted position, all while drawing my bow, picking a spot, and sending my arrow straight through it.

But I had to wait until just the right moment. I knew the deer had to be quartering away from me enough that when I stood, it wouldn't see me. Mr. Forrest had warned me that they almost have eyes in the back of their head. And so, I sat motionless for several more steps.

When I was as sure as I could be, based on what I could see through the brush, that the deer's eyes would no longer see me if I stood, I took a deep breath and then did everything I needed to do in one smooth motion. After reaching full draw, I held for maybe a second at the corner of my mouth, making sure I was locked onto the spot I wanted to hit. And then, almost without me knowing it, the arrow was on its way.

From the time I released the arrow until the time it hit the deer, it was almost as if everything was in slow motion. Things slowed down so much that my eyes easily tracked the pink feathers of the arrow as they arched slightly upwards before the broadhead landed hard into the side of the deer—right where I was looking. And I watched as those pink feathers bounded off with the deer, helping me track where it ran.

Once the deer was out of my sight, I had to sit down. I was shaking uncontrollably. When Mr. Forrest had made his way to me, I couldn't even make my mouth work. But his was running nonstop.

"You did it! You did it! You did it perfectly!" he said somewhere between a whisper and a shout. "You stalked that deer like a pro!" he continued. "Like an absolute pro!"

I still couldn't believe it. And I still couldn't talk. So, Mr. Forrest continued on.

"And the shot! It was perfect. I heard it crash not fifty yards that way," he said as he pointed in the direction the deer had run. "Let's give it a few minutes, just to be sure, and we'll make our way over to it."

It took me a few more minutes before I settled down enough to talk. My shaking didn't stop, but my expression definitely turned into a smile. I had done it. I had really done it. And what I had done was something most hunters would never do. I had stalked within fifteen yards of a deer and shot it with a bow I had made for myself.

I had killed it with nothing more than a stick and a string.

# Chapter 46

When we made our way to it, we were surprised to see that it wasn't a doe. It was a spike. And while most people wouldn't think much of a pair of spike antlers on their wall, I'm not sure I'll ever have a better trophy. It certainly was, and may always be, my biggest accomplishment.

My dad couldn't believe it when he saw us dragging the spike to the truck. He came running toward us like we were pulling a million dollars behind us. "No way! No way!" he was shouting. "I can't believe it! You did it, Parker. Oh, my heavens, you did it!" he continued screaming as he ran our way, nearly knocking over both me and Mr. Forrest when he got to us.

---

On the way home, I begged my dad to let me have his phone so that I could call and tell the Hunt Club Kids. Of course, they were as excited as I was—that was no surprise. But it was a surprise to see the three of them jumping out of Jet's dad's truck when we turned into our driveway.

They all had their bows. And they all promised they would get a deer the way I had done one day, too—the traditional way. When I looked at Mr. Forrest, he couldn't have been happier—or prouder.

Of course, my mom and sister ran out and joined in on the celebration. My mom gave me a big hug and whispered into my ear, "I knew you could do it. I just knew you could. Promise me you'll never give up on anything. Promise me," she said again as she pulled away from me, looking for an an-swer.

I nodded and said, "I promise. Thank you for not letting me quit."

———————

That night, I was almost too excited to go to bed. We all were. And so, we stayed up late, with everyone listening as I told the story again and again. But eventually, it was time for bed. "We have church in the morning," my mom kept reminding us.

As I was falling asleep, I heard my door creak the way it does when it's opening. When I looked up, my dad was walking in.

"Hey, Dad," I said without sitting up.

"Hey, son," he answered while kneeling down beside me. "I just wanted you to know how proud I am of you. I am so very proud."

I knew exactly how he felt.

"I'm proud of you too, Dad. I am so very proud of you."

# About the Author

Dr. Jimmy Tidmore is a husband, father, and pastor serving at a small church in Huntsville, Alabama. He and his son, Jet, enjoy pursuing hunting and outdoor adventures together. These adventures serve as the basis and inspiration for his books.

# Thanks for reading!

If you enjoyed *Sticks and Strings*, make sure to join the club at <u>HuntClubKids.com</u>. Also, be sure to check out each of the other books in The Hunt Club Kids Series.

Made in the USA
Las Vegas, NV
24 December 2024

15309318R00154